BY2GIRL

TERENCE BLACKER

ANDERSEN PRESS

This edition published in 2017 by
Andersen Press Limited
20 Vauxhall Bridge Road
London SW1V 2SA
www.andersenpress.co.uk

First published by Macmillan Children's Books, 2004

2 4 6 8 10 9 7 5 3 1

British Library Cataloguing in Publication Data available.

ISBN 978 1 78344 575 2

Printed and bound in Great Britain by Clays Limited,
Bungay, Suffolk, NR35 1ED

TO MARION LLOYD

If this story was a Doors song,
which would it be?

'Strange Days'?

'Ship of Fools'?

'Take It As It Comes'?

Maybe 'Wild Child' would do it . . .

1

Matthew Burton

I need you to hold it in your head, this picture of Sam Lopez when he first arrived at my front door. Keep it there while later, prettier pictures appear – Sam in a ponytail, Sam teaching Elena and the gang American football in the playground, Sam singing in his precious girl band, Sam, the ultimate class cutie.

Because this, I want you to remember, is the real, the true Sam Lopez.

He stood there, a beat-up duffel bag slung over his shoulder, in a coat about three sizes too big for him, baggy jeans sagging on to the step. His face was a wisp of paleness behind a curtain of lank, shoulder-length hair.

'Hi, Matthew.' My mother, standing just behind him, wore the strained, I'm-not-panicking-really-I'm-not look on her face that I know so well. 'This is your famous cousin Sam.'

As I muttered a greeting, my cousin pushed past me, close enough for me to notice a) how small he was and b) that he hadn't had a wash for a while.

'Let me take your coat, Sam,' said my father, who had been hovering behind me in the hallway, but he was ignored too as the newcomer ambled through to the kitchen. When we followed him in, he was looking about, almost sniffing the air like some kind of rat.

'So this is my new home,' he said, his voice hoarse but surprisingly high-pitched.

I remember how once, when my mother was talking about Sam's mother, my Aunt Galaxy, she had referred to Sam as 'an accident'. I hadn't quite understood what she meant at the time but now, standing in the kitchen, I saw it clear enough.

This was what an accident looked like – an accident in human form, an accident about to happen.

Mrs Burton

I have never been more glad to be back home. When I saw Matthew, trying to look pleased at the arrival of his American cousin, and dear David in the hall, his polite, social smile in place, I almost burst into tears.

It had been a terrible trip. The funeral, the meeting with the lawyer, the journey back across the Atlantic with a moody, traumatised thirteen-year-old. It was not going to be easy dealing with Sam, but at least now I was back with my own little family. Together, we would make this thing work.

Matthew

Eight days ago, life had been simple. The summer holidays had just started. I was kind of whacked out after the long term and was ready for many, many mornings lying in my bed, afternoons with my friends, evenings slobbing out in front of the TV.

Then the news came through from America. My mother's younger sister, Galaxy, had been involved in a serious car crash. One moment she was in a bad way, the next she was in a coma, the next she was dead. Mum flew out for the funeral.

I knew I should feel upset about the whole dead-aunt thing but, since I had never met Galaxy and she had only been mentioned now and then by my parents in a slightly embarrassed and jokey way, she had never exactly featured in my life so far. In fact, all I knew was that she sounded decidedly weird.

Mrs Burton

My sister Gail became Galaxy at a rebirthing ceremony at the Glastonbury Festival when she was eighteen. She had always liked to be different from the rest of us.

A couple of years later, she went on holiday to America with a bunch of long-haired friends. When they came back, she stayed, having hitched up with Tod Strange, the lead guitarist of a rather unpleasant heavy-metal band called 666.

We lost touch with Galaxy until just after I got married and was pregnant with Matthew, when she sent me a postcard. Tod was history, she said. These days she was with a guy called Tony Lopez, a nightclub owner. Oh, and guess what? She was going to have a baby.

So we each started a family at more or less the same time – me in a house in suburban London, Aunt Galaxy, as she now was, roaming around America in a camper van. We received the odd card from her – photographs of her little boy, Sam, odd scraps of news. After a couple of years, she told us that Tony Lopez had left home 'to go travel and find himself', as she put it. Later we heard that he was in jail.

We kept in touch down the years, but the truth was that we had less and less in common; Galaxy living on the west coast with what we always imagined to be a rather undesirable crowd, us living our quiet but busy lives in London.

And then came the big, the terrible news.

I was surprised to find how upset I was. My sister and I had never been particularly close as children and, when she grew into this rather strange and irresponsible adult who was different from me in every way, I came to think of her almost as a stranger who had just happened to have been born into the same family as me by some kind of odd accident.

Now I realised that I would miss my sister and her weird ways. Flying out to America for the funeral, I thought not of Galaxy, the rock chick with her dubious friends, but of Gail, the little girl who was never quite in step with the rest of the world but saw that as the world's

4

problem, not hers. In spite of having my own lovely, close family, I felt lonely without her.

In San Diego, where she had been living most recently, I was met by a man called Jeb Durkowitz who turned out to be Galaxy's lawyer. He told me that things were somewhat complicated. Sam, who had just turned thirteen, was alone in the world. In a letter to Durkowitz, Galaxy had made it clear that, should anything happen to her, the Burton family should look after him.

Poor Gail, poor Galaxy. Even in death, she had a talent for causing trouble.

Matthew

My cousin stank, and I sensed that he didn't care that he stank. It was as if smelling to high heaven was a way of showing right from the start that he just didn't care what people thought of him.

He sat, slumped on one of the kitchen stools, gazing at his new family, his small, button-like eyes dark and glistening.

'So,' he said. 'Mr and Mrs David Burton. At home. With their only son, Matthew.'

As he spoke, it seemed to me that there was more contempt in that American drawl of his than seemed exactly right or polite in a kid of his age.

I glanced at my parents, expecting some kind of cool put-down, but they both stood smiling at this hairball idiot as if he were the most special and adorable thing they had ever seen in their entire lives.

Eventually, my father turned to me. 'Maybe Sam would like a juice from the fridge,' he said.

'Juice sucks,' said Sam.

Dad smiled. 'Fair enough,' he said reasonably.

We soon discovered that everything sucked, according to Sam Lopez.

Driving around London to see the sights sucked. The meals that my father cooked for us sucked. All four of the Pantuccis from next door, who called in to say hello, sucked. British TV sucked big time ('You got no cable? No digital?' he said. 'Please tell me you're kidding.'). Going to bed at any time before midnight sucked, as did getting up at any time before midday.

By the second day, this attitude was beginning to get to me. 'How come everything in your life sucks?' I asked him over dinner.

He turned to me, his eyes wide and dark, and I realised too late that it had not exactly been the best thing to say to someone whose mum had just died.

'Search me, cuz,' he said quietly. 'I ask myself the same question every day.'

Mr Burton

It was a difficult time. We have always been a family that likes to deal with problems by talking them through together, but Sam preferred his own company. He spent hours in his room, alone, listening to music though his headphones or he sat in front of the TV, staring blankly at the screen.

When he did speak, it was often in a harsh, angry tone of voice that tore through what was once the easy atmosphere of the house like someone ripping fabric. He had an alarming turn of phrase for a boy of his age too. Sam may not have had much of an education but, when it came to creative swearing, he was pretty near to the top of the class.

But the way I saw it was this: the silences, the moods, the outbursts, the bad language were all a cry for help from a kid in pain. It was the duty of the Burton family to help Sam through this dark, dark time.

Matthew

A word about my parents. To an outsider – Sam Lopez, say – they might have seemed kind of topsy-turvy. As long as I can remember, Mum has been the main wage-earner, working in an employment agency at a job which gives her a daily nervous breakdown.

My father works part-time from home, checking documents as a proofreader for a law firm, but his real love, his career almost, is looking after the home. Dad's version of housework is not the quick, what-the-hell-it'll-do version of most men – he really and genuinely takes pride in keeping things sparkling and clean. He is the true, official article: a house husband. He can spend a whole afternoon on a family meal. He has a special day for vacuuming. He can wear an apron without embarrassment. Now and then I watch him hanging clothes out on the line, carefully, slowly, the pegs between his teeth, and I just know that this, the family and the family home, are what matters to him more than any job or career.

Look at it this way. I have a mixed-up version of a so-called traditional family – not so much Dad and Mum as Mad and Dum.

Elena Griffiths

For me, it was not the summer of Sam Lopez at all. It was the summer of hope, of romance, of secrets, of planning for a new future. It was the summer of Mark Kramer.

At Bradbury Hill School, everybody knew Mark. The boys wanted to be him. They tried to grow their hair long and floppy like his. They wore his style of clothes, liked the brands that he liked. Some of them (truly, sadly, tragically) imitated his smile, his sleepy way of talking.

And the girls? Obviously, they just wanted to date him.

Maybe I was kidding myself – I was going into my second year, he was soon-to-be king of the Lower Sixth – but, when he started talking to me while we were both queuing for lunch during the last week of term, I honestly thought it meant something. He had been chatting to Justin, a friend of his, about the new Cameron Diaz film they were planning to see. As it happened, I had just seen a preview (my mum's in the business), so I casually mentioned that the film was OK. In fact, it was almost good.

Mark looked at me in that gentle, aristocratic way of his, as if seeing me for the first time, and asked me how come I knew so much about a film that had not been released. I told him that my mum was a casting director. In fact, she had met Cameron a couple of times at showbiz parties (which is true). Cameron was really nice, I said – very, you know, normal.

'Showbiz parties, eh?' Mark laughed and his friend laughed too. He said he was going to see the film the following Saturday, and I mentioned I wouldn't mind catching it again.

'Cool,' he said.

Maybe I read too much into that look, into that 'Cool', but at that moment it seemed clear. Something secret and magical had passed between us – something which made words sort of irrelevant. I was going on a date with Mark Kramer, the date he had just set up without revealing our plan to Justin.

It was big news, a socko moment of the major kind. Normally, I would share any secret with my best friends, Charley and Zia, but this was different. They would either make fun of me or they would be jealous.

I so didn't need that right then.

Matthew

At that moment in my summer holidays, it seemed as if nothing was going to be good or simple or normal ever again. When our home had just been Mum, Dad and me, we had known where we were – like any family, we had our fights and rows and days when things were a bit rocky, but we had been around each other long enough to know, by instinct, how to straighten things out. We understood when you need to talk and when to keep quiet, when to say sorry – all the usual parent-kid stuff.

But when three became four, and the extra person had more rage and unhappiness in him than the rest of us put together, the whole balance became skewed. I would hear Mum and Dad having hissed, secretive conversations about Sam. Their smiles became forced and phoney. Everything they said and thought seemed to revolve around my cousin and how he was coming to terms with his new, motherless life.

Beside that great, throbbing tragedy, the everyday stuff of my little world suddenly seemed kind of puny and insignificant.

As for Sam, he had learned a useful lesson – being an orphan gives you power. So while my parents were around, he would do his silent 'n' moody act. Then, as soon as we were alone, he would set about winding me up.

We were sitting in front of the TV one afternoon, when he looked out of the window and noticed my father washing the car in the front drive.

'What is it with that guy?' he murmured, just loudly enough for me to hear.

I made the mistake of responding. 'You mean my father?'

'Always cleaning things and scrubbing and dusting. Has he got some kind of psycho hang-up?'

I stared at the TV, now determined not to be suckered into a row.

Sam turned to me. 'Do you believe in reincarnation?'

I shrugged.

'Because I was thinking, maybe your dad was a butler in a previous life. Or a cleaning lady.'

I clenched my teeth and said nothing.

'Now my dad – he wouldn't know what dusting was,' Sam said suddenly. 'He's so cool that just hearing about him would blow you away. Your brain couldn't take it in.'

I stared ahead in silence.

'You wouldn't believe the stuff we did together.' Sam chuckled and shook his head. 'Yup, he was a real father, you know?'

Without a word, I stood up, walked out of the room and outside the house to join my father. I'm not crazy about car-washing, but it was the only way I could show Sam where my loyalty lay.

'I'm not sure I can take much more of this,' I told Dad.

'He'll settle down when he goes to school.'

I groaned. 'I can't believe he's going to be in my class. It's going to be a nightmare, Dad.'

My father looked over the car, a sponge in his hand, and said the words which made my heart sink every time I heard them.

'Maybe it's time Sam met a few of your friends.'

Tyrone Sherman

We were in the park, at our normal place by the shed, waiting for Matt's famous American cousin.

He was late. According to Matt, he was late for everything.

'Maybe he doesn't exist at all,' said Jake. 'Maybe he's Matt's imaginary friend.'

'I wish,' said Matt.

Time passed. Jake kicked a football against the wall of the shed. Matt and I watched the world go by, just like we had done a thousand times before. This was our territory. It may have been just a shelter in a children's playground, but the three of us had been hanging out here for five years or so. In the early days, we would come here to take cover if it rained while we were on the swings or the slide. Now, we just sat and talked. Even if we were given the odd cold stare now and then by parents in the playground or passing by on their way to the public toilets around the back of the building, we didn't care. This was our own private place.

When we were kids, we had taken to calling ourselves the Shed Gang half as a joke and half seriously. Somehow, the name had stuck.

'Here we go,' Matt said suddenly.

I followed the direction of his eyes.

Turning into the park was a small, long-haired kid. 'That's him?' I asked. 'Bit of a titch, isn't he?'

'And get a load of that hair,' said Jake.

'It's like I told you,' said Matt. 'He's a hippy.'

'Looks more like a girl to me,' said Jake.

And Matt laughed. 'You wait,' he said.

Matthew

He swaggered towards us, his T-shirt and jeans and blond hair billowing behind him as if he were a very small ship under sail. When he reached where we stood, he slowed down and wandered up to us, hands in pockets. 'How ya doin'?' he said, flashing one of his rare smiles. 'I'm Sam Lopez.'

Tyrone and Jake mumbled a greeting.

'So this is the famous shed.' Sam sat down on the bench and looked around him. I was expecting one of his trademark put-downs, but instead he clicked his teeth in a sort of approving way. 'It's OK.'

'We like it,' I said coldly.

'So what goes on round here?'

'Not much,' said Tyrone.

'D'you play football?' Jake asked.

Sam glanced at the ball at Jake's feet. 'You mean soccer? In the States, it's a girl's game.'

'That's because in the States, you can't play it.' Jake kicked the ball hard against the wall.

'Sure we could if we wanted to.' Sam reached over, took Tyrone's phone and casually worked the game with his thumb. 'Thing is, we prefer real football.' He handed the phone back. 'There you go, you're on to the next level,' he said casually.

He stood up, spat on his hand and caught the ball as it came back off the wall. He held it for a second or two, then flipped it over. For a moment, the ball stuck to his hand before it fell.

'Take a look.' Sam stood in front of Jake, rolling his

shoulders in relaxed, limbering-up movement. 'This,' he said, 'is football.' He bent at the knees, holding an imaginary ball in both hands, with arms outstretched. 'Two! Sixty-five!' He yelled the numbers so loud that the mothers across the playground looked up to see what was going on.

And suddenly Sam was off, dancing and jinking across the tarmac, shoulder-barging imaginary players aside, half-turning to take a long pass, then sprinting onwards for a few yards until, just past the seesaws, he made to throw the ball in the air in triumph.

'Touchdown!' he screamed. 'We haaaaaave a ball game.'

He danced along beside the metal fence, head thrown back, his little legs and arms punching upwards in crazed celebration like a demented, long-haired goblin.

We laughed. There was no other reaction.

'Nutter,' said Jake.

'What planet is that guy from?' said Tyrone.

Sam returned to us and slumped down on the bench, breathing hard. 'That's what you call football,' he said. 'It's better with a ball, of course.'

Jake shook his head. 'You are one crazy Yank.'

'You ain't seen nuttin' yet.' Sam wiped his nose with the back of his sleeve.

Mrs Cartwright

You don't become a head teacher of a large school without learning how to what I call roll with the punches, but when Mrs Burton, the mother of one of our younger boys, Matthew, rang with the news about his American cousin, I can't say I was overly optimistic about our ability to help with a schooling facility.

Bradbury Hill is over-subscribed – we are a very, very successful school – and the idea of an American child turning up out of the blue at the start of our second year seemed like a bit of a non-starter to me.

But Mrs Burton is a very determined woman. She explained how Sam was alone in the world, exactly the same age as Matthew. She suggested that Bradbury Hill might gain some useful publicity mileage from the whole business.

Publicity mileage. I'll be truthful here. That spoke to me.

As it happened, there was a gap in Year Eight which this Sam person could usefully occupy. Even when Mrs Burton explained that no reports were available to Sam because the mother – something of a hopeless case, by all accounts – had moved her child from school to school so often, I failed to hear the alarm bells in my brain.

I blame myself on this one. I simply should have been what I call more careful.

2

Charley Johnson

We're close, we bitches. When we were at primary school, there was one unspoken rule – if you upset one of us, you had all of us to answer to.

Elena Griffiths, Zia Khan and Charley Johnson. We were like the different sides of one all-conquering personality. Apart, each of us was nothing special. Together we were unbeatable.

Elena was pretty, skinny, kind of ditsy, a bit too hung up on the whole celebrity business to be entirely normal.

Zia was part of this big, successful Asian family. Somewhere along the line she had learned that silence, the whole little-mouse thing, was as good a method of getting your own way as the louder approach that Elena and I use. Sensitivity, charm and a talent for playing the guitar – who could be surprised that Zia is top of the charts when it comes to Teacher's Pet awards? And no one ever suspects that behind the innocent facade lurks the true Ms Khan – scheming, wild and dangerous.

I envy her the charm thing. It seems that I'm too big, too loud for that kind of stuff. On the other hand, I have been top of every class that I've attended and who needs charm if you have brains?

Zia Khan

Elena broke the golden rule that summer. It was the one about boys.

Boys, we had decided when we were about nine, were a waste of time. Our enemies were a sad trio who called themselves (I promise I'm not making this up) 'the Shed Gang'. They annoyed us and we gained our revenge by getting them into trouble at every opportunity. This was not difficult – they were boys, after all.

When the Sheds – Jake, Tyrone and Matt – started calling us names, we took their favourite word for us, turned it into a compliment and made it our own gang name. The Bitches.

All was just fine and dandy with the three of us until Elena decided to fall for the love god of the Lower Sixth, Mark Kramer.

Jake Smiley

You want the truth? I didn't mind him at first. Matt had been telling us these horror stories about his cousin over the past few days and I admit the guy looked a bit of a fright, but when he did that crazy jig around the playground the first time we met, it occurred to me that he might be a pain but at least he would liven things up.

Summer holidays can sometimes drag. You sit around, you check out new video games, you chat, but then what? The answer to the question was that we found out more about Sam Lopez.

There was something about the American that shook up our little group, that made us talk about ourselves in a way that we normally never did.

Why? Because, however strange and out of whack our lives might have seemed, it was nothing to what Sam had on offer.

So, as he was catching his breath after his American football exhibition, he chatted about how he had played back home at one of his schools.

'How many schools have you been to?' I asked.

Sam frowned, and counted on his fingers for a moment, then shrugged. 'Twelve? Thirteen? My mom and I moved around a bit. Something like that.'

Tyrone whistled, impressed.

'Matt said she was a bit wild,' he said.

Sam gave a little gasp, which might have been surprise or pain.

'Tyrone means wild in a good way,' said Matt quickly. The American smiled, then began to laugh softly. 'That was Mom all right,' he said. 'Wiiiiild.'

And so we started talking. There was something about the stranger's, whole dead-mother, multi-school situation that seemed to make it easier to open up about ourselves.

I talked about how my mum and dad had split up last year, how I felt out of place at home with just my mother and my older sister. I saw Dad once a week but that was no picnic either. We'd go to a film or sit in a restaurant, making small talk about everything except what was really on our minds. Suddenly, it was as if we were strangers.

Tyrone chipped in with the story about how he had never met his father on account of his having taken a holiday back in the West Indies soon after he was born and never came back. He talked about his weight problem – how they used to call him 'Jumbo' and 'the Tank' at school, how his mum was forever trying new diets on him, how they made him feel weak and ill but never worked.

Matt even joined in, fessing up that he felt embarrassed when his dad did the housework and went around in an apron or when his mother rang up the school to complain about something or other.

'Loser City, man.' Sam winked and there was something so easy and grown-up about his manner that the three of us found ourselves laughing. 'So,' he said. 'What do you guys do for kicks around here?'

Elena

I'm not going into the Mark Kramer thing. The way I see it, what happened (what didn't happen) between me and Mark has nothing to do with anybody. It's simply not relevant. End of story.

All right, maybe you need to know a little, just the basics. I showed up for the Cameron Diaz film that Saturday. So did Mark. When he walked into the foyer, I went up to him, blushing sweetly beneath the make-up that had taken me about two hours to put on. Then I saw Tasha, a girl from his class, was behind him. She linked her hand through his arm and for what seem like half a lifetime the three of us stood staring at one another, each of us lost for words.

Eventually, it was Tasha who broke the silence. 'And your problem is?' she said.

I turned and ran, through the swing doors, out into the night. I hated Tasha, I hated myself but, above all else, I hated Mark Kramer. In fact, I hated all boys.

So maybe, come to think of it, the whole thing wasn't quite as irrelevant as I thought.

Matthew

Over the next few days, as we showed Sam around what he insisted on calling 'the hood', he talked about his life back home. The way he told it, every day was spent hanging out with bike gangs, cruising the projects, getting into fights, and every night he was backstage at some rock concert with his good old mum.

We listened to these stories, trying not to look impressed. Until then, we had liked to think that we three were tough enough to handle ourselves should things get a little iffy in the park, on the streets, or in the school playground. We were as bad and hard as it took for teachers now and then to express concern to our parents about our 'attitude problems'.

But Sam, if half of his tales from back home were true, was in a different league of badness, harder than we even wanted to be. In San Diego, his posse shoplifted for fun. They nicked cars, carried knives. They had frenzied, bloody gang fights, just like in the movies. They were known to the police.

The more we heard about the wild and wacky world of Sam and his posse, the less comfortable we felt with him. Either he was a lying fantasist or he was a mini-criminal. Whatever, he was trouble – and each of us had quite enough trouble of our own to be going on with.

And that was before the bust-up at Burger Bill's.

Burger Bill

If I had my way, I'd ban all kids between the ages of twelve and eighteen. They're nothing but trouble, particularly the boys.

Particularly those boys.

Matthew

We were sitting there in this cafe called Burger Bill's, when Jake started talking about his dad. Mr Smiley had been missing custody visits with Jake recently and now it looked as if father and son would be meeting up even less often.

Two nights previously, Mr Smiley had been driving back to his flat after a business dinner when his car had been stopped by the police. He had been breathalysed, failed the test and been kept at the police station all night.

I noticed that, as we talked about all this, expressing our sympathy, Sam was unusually silent. He looked around him, drumming the Formica table with his fingers as if nothing could bore him more than the story of Jake's dad.

'So what happens round here if you drive when you're on the sauce?' he asked out of the blue. 'You get slammed up or what?'

'Mr Smiley could lose his licence for a while,' I said.

'And my dad needs his car to get over to see me,' Jake added miserably.

Sam sniffed. 'Excuse me while I cry,' he said.

We all looked at him in surprise. He sat back in his chair and raised both hands. 'Hey, face it, it's no biggie,' he said. 'So Jake's old man spent a night in the pen and can't drive for a while. Big tragedy.'

Jake leaned forward over the table. 'Don't push it,' he said. 'This isn't a joke.'

'Who's joking?' Sam ran his fingers through his hair and tugged at it in a distinctly unfriendly gesture. 'You know, Jake, I think you're in danger of confusing me with someone who gives a good goddam what happens to your daddy.'

'Easy, Sam,' said Tyrone.

But Sam continued to stare deep into Jake's eyes. 'You see, when you have a dad who's spent most of his life in the slammer, who's there right now, then the idea of someone spending a few hours behind bars...' He shrugged. 'Well, it doesn't exactly break my heart.'

'Sheesh,' said Tyrone. 'What did your dad do?'

Sam shrugged. 'Stuff. That's what he did. Big stuff. When I was born he had a few nightclubs. He got involved in a few things that maybe weren't strictly on the level. One night he fell out with a colleague. The colleague had an accident. He got kind of smeared. Dad took the rap. Like I say – stuff.'

He had done it again. Even when something unusually dramatic had happened in one of our lives, Sam managed to come up with something bigger, scarier and more dramatic.

'That's...' Bravely, Tyrone was trying to find the right words for one of those tricky occasions when you discover that your friend's dad is in jail for murder. 'That's... I mean, that's really terrible.'

'It's the way it goes, ole buddy.' Sam slurped at his drink through a straw. 'My old man ain't been around since I was five years old. Now and then I'd hear about his latest little scrape with the law from my mom. She'd make a joke of it – she called it the Crash Bulletin.'

'Crash?' said Tyrone.

'That's his name. His real name's Tony but, what with all the busts and accidents and stuff, everyone calls him Crash – Crash Lopez.' Sam spoke the words with pride.

There was silence for a moment. Then Jake seemed to tune into the conversation for the first time in a while.

'Crash,' he said, and I could tell from the look on his face that he was still angry about what Sam had said about his father. 'Bit of a weird name, isn't it?'

Sam looked warily surprised. 'Waddya mean weird?'
Jake laughed. 'What's he got – a couple of brothers called Bang and Wallop?'

Sam gave a sort of yelp of rage and, before we could do anything, he was out of his seat, lunging across the table, scattering the polystyrene cups, his hands pummelling at Jake's face.

'Don't diss my dad!' he was screaming. 'Diss my dad and you die!'

Bill, a fat, sweaty guy who is the manager of the burger bar, hurried over and pulled Sam off Jake. Ignoring the American's screams and curses, he marched him to the door and threw him out as if he were a stray cat. He locked the door, then walked back to the table.

He looked down, resting two meaty fists on the table. 'What are your names, you three?' he asked.

'Smith,' said Tyrone. 'We're all called Smith.'

Bill stood there for a moment, as if considering what to do next. Then he walked briskly back to the door and unlocked it. 'Get out,' he said with a jerk of his head. 'And don't come back unless you want me to take you down to the police station myself.'

We scurried past him, Jake with a hand over his eye.

Outside we looked around us. The shopping precinct was deserted. There was no sign anywhere of the crazy son of Crash Lopez.

Tyrone

I was scared, and I'd lay money that Matt and Jake were scared too. It was one of those occasions where events slide out of control and suddenly you feel lost, helpless and small.

We wandered down the empty precinct until we were a safe distance from Burger Bill's. 'I don't believe that,' said Matt, his voice shaky.

Jake sniffed and wiped his nose. 'It was only a joke,' he said.

I shook my head. 'He's too much, that Sam. All those schools and gangs, his mum in a car crash and now his dad turns out to be some kind of psycho killer.'

'He says,' muttered Jake.

'It's not his fault, I suppose,' said Matt.

'It's not ours, either!' It was an angry wail that came from Jake. 'Just because his life's a mess, why does he need to mess up ours too? I've got enough problems without this.'

His voice echoed off the shop windows, around the concrete walls. And at that moment of despair, we suddenly found that we were not alone.

Charley

Good luck, bad luck, whatever, we were in that precinct that night too.

We were planning to see Ratz, some kind of rodent-based animated feature, at the cinema complex and had decided to grab a Coke at Burger Bill's before we went.

As we came up the escalator, we found a very sorry group indeed. It was the Sheds and they seemed to be upset about something.

We smiled when we saw them. All right, that's not quite true. We laughed. I'm sorry, but it would take a heart of stone not to find humour in the sight of Conk, Ears and the Tank – better known to their friends (if they had friends) as Jake, Matt and Tyrone.

Jake used to look quite normal at our last school but, over the past year, he's grown in all the wrong directions. It's as if parts of his body – arms, legs, ears, nose, even his hair – were in some kind of race away from him, all heading in different directions. There are no prizes for guessing who the winner was in this race – Jake's nose is a sight to behold. It was Zia who gave him a new nickname – Concorde, or Conk, for short.

Matt looks kind of normal but there is something creepy about him – the way he says little but always seems to be listening and watching whatever is going on from the sideline. He'll probably grow up to be a spy, earwigging for a living.

As for Tyrone, he's all right but there is no escaping the fact that he's a serious scale-buster. I'm no skeleton but I tell you, beside the Tank I feel virtually invisible.

Any other time, we might just have passed them by but, for reasons we only discovered later, Elena was out for blood that night.

'Look what the cat's brought in,' she said loudly as we approached them. The three boys ignored her. 'How are the old Sheds doing?' she said.

'Leave it, Elena.' This was Tyrone. 'We're looking for someone.'

'What, someone to be your friend?' said Zia, entering into the spirit of it. 'You'll be lucky.'

It was at that point that I noticed that Jake was lurking behind the other two. He had a hand over his right eye.

'Been in a fight, have you?' I asked.

'No,' Jake muttered. 'I...bumped into a door.'

Elena started laughing again. 'That's the trouble with sheds,' she said. 'They get banged by doors.'

She ambled past them, towards Burger Bill's, and we followed her.

Elena

I'll admit this much. I shouldn't have done what I did. But I was in a really bad mood. Somebody had to pay.

Bill was wiping one of the tables.

'Hi, Bill,' I said. 'Looks like the Messy Eaters Club has been here.'

Bill muttered something about banning anyone under sixteen from his bar. As he straightened up to let us take our seats, he nodded outside, where Conk and the gang had been a moment ago.

'Little yobs,' he said. 'If I had their names, I'd sort them out for good and all.'

'Names?' I said. 'I think I might be able to help you there.'

PC Chivers

I have a record that we received a call at the station from the proprietor of a local hamburger establishment, a Mr William Patterson. The desk sergeant requested me to pay a visit to the families of the boys alleged to be involved in the incident. As it happens, it was the first time that I had been required to handle a domestic without the aid of a colleague. To my recollection, it was a straightforward caution job, which went off without a hitch. Beyond that I am unable to comment.

Mrs Burton

It was at about this time that our lives began to seem like some sort of mad soap opera.

One evening, just after I had returned from work, we had a visit from a policeman. He was not a very impressive policeman, it was true – he was barely out of his teens and had yet to grow into his uniform – but his appearance on our doorstep was enough to get the neighbours talking. The police are not often seen in Somerton Gardens.

He told me that his visit was in connection with an affray at a local eating establishment. One of those involved was a certain Matthew Burton.

3

Matthew

We got the blame. Can you believe that? Sam goes psycho, and it's Jake, Tyrone and me who get cautioned by the police. It was too much.

After the policeman left and Mum and Dad had finished giving me the full parental interrogation, I went upstairs. It was time for me and Sam Lopez to have a little talk.

His door was closed. I pushed it open without knocking.

Sam had changed the spare room, just like he changed everything else. A few days ago, this had been a fresh, clean, sunny room. Now it was a den. The curtains were drawn. The floor was a tangle of clothes and old rock magazines. The air was thick with the whiff of ancient socks.

He was on the bed, playing a game on his phone that he had brought with him from America. Lying there, frowning with concentration, he looked small and innocent, nothing like the fist-of-fury psycho we had seen at Burger Bill's.

'Trouble?' he murmured without taking his eyes off the screen. 'I could swear I heard raised voices in the

Burton household.'

'A policeman called round. It was about a fight at Burger Bill's.'

Sam chuckled. 'I guess the old Sheds are known to the police now too.'

'Yeah, right. Thanks for that.'

'The dude insulted my family.' Sam spoke in a bored sing-song voice. 'In my book, that counts as a capital offence. He's lucky he can still walk.'

'And in my book a person can make a joke without getting his face punched in.'

'Different strokes for different folks,' Sam said casually. 'I guess he won't be making fun of my dad from now on.'

I gave him my chilliest smile. 'That's true,' I said. 'Because you won't be around.'

'Huh?' A tiny frown of concentration gathered above Sam's dark eyes. 'Why's that then?'

'Find your own gang, Sam. We don't need the hassle.'

Sam laid down his phone. 'Hey, come on, Matthew. These things happen in gangs. I got slapped by guys in my posse loads of times. It goes with the territory.'

'Yeah, well, it's as you say – different strokes for different folks.'

'What about when I go to your school?'

'There are loads of other kids. You'll be fine.'

Sam gazed ahead of him. On a shelf at the end of his bed he had put three framed photographs. There was a picture of him with his mum sitting outside some kind of tepee thing, and a publicity photograph of the rock band 666 in which Galaxy could be seen kneeling at the feet of a long-haired guitarist. Then, in a small plastic frame, there was a shot of Galaxy with a baby in her arms. Beside them, a big, cheesy grin on his face, was a small, dark-haired guy. I guessed it was the one and only Crash.

'I don't want to be alone.' Sam spoke the words so quietly that he might have been speaking a private thought out loud.

'Maybe you should have thought of that before you mashed Jake's face.'

'I don't want to be alone, Matt.' When he repeated the words, there was an echo of desperation in his voice.

He turned and looked up at me, unblinking, dark-eyed, and for the first time I saw something different and unfamiliar in Sam Lopez – something that he had managed to keep concealed until now. He was afraid. He was lost. All his life, the people who mattered to him had left. Every time he had begun to feel secure, something had shifted, changed, and suddenly there he had been, all alone once more. Sam may have come on like this big tough guy but, behind the mask, he was one scared kid.

'Could you just tell Jake and Ty that I'm really sorry about what happened?' he said. 'Tell them I'd do anything to make it right.'

'Like what?'

He sat up on his bed. 'In the States, new gang members have to do some kind of initiation test to prove that they deserve to be in the gang.' A note of confidence, more like the old Sam, had entered his voice. 'So for my initiation I could get stuff from the shops for you. Hot-wire a car and take you for a ride. I know – I could get back at the guys who finked on us to the cops. Show them that nobody messes with us Sheds and gets away with it.'

'I'll talk to Jake and Tyrone,' I said. 'But I wouldn't hold out your hopes.'

'Thanks, Matt.'

'Anyway,' I said, 'I've got a sneaky feeling the guys who finked on us to the cops weren't guys at all.'

Zia

What Elena did at Burger Bill's cast a bit of a shadow over the holidays. At the time, Charley and I must have looked shocked by the cool way she had given Bill the names of the boys because, as we sat across from her at the table, she started crying.

This, with Elena, is a sure sign that she has something to hide.

Behind the counter Bill was on the phone, and we just knew that his threat to report Jake and the other two to the police had been real. Charley got into this lecture about how Elena had gone too far, how there was a big difference between getting someone into trouble at school and with the police.

Then it all came out – the Great Mark Kramer Disaster.

Well, excuse me, we were not impressed. Elena makes a prat of herself with a minor-league hunk and, to make herself feel better, she drops three boys, who had nothing to do with anything, into the doo-doo.

I told her I thought she was sad.

'Beyond sad,' Charley agreed. 'Tragic.'

And that was it. Elena swore at us and walked out of Burger Bill's.

We never did get to see *Ratz*.

Matthew

Why? *Why?* Even before they reported us to the police, I would now and then wonder why exactly we were at war with Charley Johnson, Elena Griffiths and Zia Khan.

We had known them ever since we had all arrived at primary school in the same year. I could swear that the three of them were absolutely fine and normal until we all reached our third or fourth year at school – I can distinctly remember us all playing football together in the playground.

So why did they turn? What happened? How was it that, at the age of about ten, they suddenly seemed to belong to another species altogether – one that was strange and hostile to all civilised life forms?

It was a mystery. All we knew was that, when the Bitches were around, there was trouble and, when there was trouble, it was never the girls who got the blame. It was us.

Then, when we all moved up to the new school, things got even worse.

It was as if our very presence at Bradbury Hill reminded them of things about themselves in the past that they wanted to forget. They wanted to be big, grown-up, but, when they took a look at us, they were somehow reminded that they were still just kids.

At first, they took to ignoring us or, as we passed, they would mutter something to one another and go away giggling. They told other members of the class that at our previous school, we were called 'the Losers' (false: everyone wanted to join our gang). They spread a rumour that Tyrone had broken a spring on the trampoline at primary school (false: he never went near the trampoline). They said that an outbreak of nits a couple of years back had been caused by me (false, or at least mostly false: lots of people had nits one term). They decided that Jake's nose was the biggest joke in history and thought up a nasty nickname for him.

But it was in Steve Forrester's class where there was the worst trouble, for here the girls knew that virtually whatever happened, the blame would never fall on them.

The way I saw it, they started the war, not us.

Steve Forrester

It is entirely wrong to suggest that I am in any way biased against the boys in my classes. It so happened that the three boys in question were a bad influence upon one another, albeit that their individual contributions to class activities were acceptable. Those three, together, were trouble. I saw it as my duty to make sure that I headed off the trouble before it became more serious.

Matthew

That tangle with the law touched each of our lives in different ways. Tyrone's mother, a tall, flashy woman, some kind of interior designer for houses, grounded him for a week. Even when things are going well, she treats her Tyrone as if he's some kind of private punishment for her, and having a policeman turn up on her doorstep was not exactly the best of times. Things were pretty bad in the Sherman household that summer. Mrs Sherman took to wondering out loud why she couldn't have had a nice normal girl rather than a boy like Tyrone – which was kind of rich when you think that it was a load of girls who had caused the problem in the first place.

For Mrs Smiley, it was another reason to blame Jake's dad, the walkout king. She hung around Jake, moaning about the many terrible things Mr Smiley had done and how it was not surprising that Jake was angry. Most evenings, according to Jake, she found comfort somewhere else – in a gin bottle.

And Mr and Mrs Burton? They were very stern and sensitive for a while before letting Sam and me get on with our lives. Normally we would go camping for a week or two, but Mum's trip to America had taken up her holiday allowance, so pretty soon the Sheds were back out there on the mean streets of suburbia.

But as far as we were concerned, Sam was history. I had mentioned my conversation with him, his idea of doing something wild and great enough to win back our friendship, but Jake was still smarting from what happened at Burger Bill's, while Tyrone was still simmering with rage about the hard time he was getting at home.

And maybe I was angrier than either of them. At that moment, it seemed to me that my cousin had stamped all over my life, my family and my friends, leaving a hopeless mess behind him for me to clear up. Jake and Tyrone could drop him from the gang, but my future with Sam Lopez stretched ahead of me like a jail sentence.

So, without ever discussing it in detail, we had come to the conclusion that we would let him tag along over the summer but, once school started, he would be on his own.

Sam sensed what was happening and took it surprisingly badly. He tried to persuade us that there was nothing wrong with a bit of fighting – it was the glue that kept a gang together, he said.

Then, time after time, he returned to the idea of some weird kind of test that would allow him to prove that he deserved to belong to the gang.

At first, we ignored him. Then we had a better idea. We'd give him his test and maybe then, when he had failed it, he would leave us alone.

All we had to do was find him one impossible task.

Tyrone

It was Matt's idea, but I helped along the way.

One night, I was talking to him on the phone. Matt was saying that there was only one way to shut Sam out once and for all – we had to set him a task that would prove, beyond the slightest shadow of doubt, that he could never be one of us.

'Yeah,' I said gloomily. 'Then he'll set up a rival gang at school. We'll have two sets of enemies – Sam and the Bitches.'

'Maybe he could join their gang,' Matt grumbled. 'After all, he looks like a girl with his cute little face and all that hair.'

'Small enough too,' I laughed. We chatted some more and then we hung up.

He rang back five minutes later, sounding unusually excited.

'Tyrone,' he said. 'I've had a thought.'

4

Matthew

We gathered at Tyrone's house.

Tyrone, Jake and I sat in three armchairs, as if we were part of a court in session. Sam strode about the room, restless and wired, joking in a tense, unfunny way. Ever since I had told him that the Sheds had thought of a way that he could work his way back into the gang, he had been sickeningly cheerful.

'OK, so show me the money, guys.' He did a little jive-dance around the room, and I noticed that Tyrone was watching him nervously. The Shermans' home was one of those houses where nothing is out of place, with no trace of a speck of dirt, where even the ornaments are carefully arranged like soldiers on parade.

'So waddya want me to do?' Sam was saying. 'Jump a train from a bridge? Lay a bit of heavy graffiti on a high-rise building? Like, "THE SHEDS RULE"?'

'Nothing as difficult as that,' I said coolly.

Sam stopped moving around for a moment. 'Not difficult? You're kidding. Gimme something really hard, man.'

'It's a bit less physical than what you were thinking of,' said Jake, whose left eye had, over the past couple of days, turned a pretty shade of purple and pink.

'I dunno,' said Tyrone, smiling. 'It's physical in a way – very physical.'

'Hey, stop jerking around, OK?' said Sam. 'Just tell me what I gotta do.'

Jake picked up a plastic shopping bag, then slowly turned it upside down. A pile of clothes tumbled out. School clothes.

School clothes for a girl.

'What's this?' Sam poked at the purple skirt with the toe of his trainer.

'It's my sister's school uniform,' said Jake.

'And?'

'And now it's yours,' said Tyrone.

'I don't get it.' Sam crouched down and laid out the clothes – the coat and skirt of a school uniform, the white shirt and socks. It was like a small body on the ground. 'Is this some kind of sad British joke?' he said.

I sat forward in my chair and spelled it out for him. 'If you want to join us, here's your initiation test. For one week, five school days, we require you to be a bit of an actor – to play a part,' I said. 'Every morning on the way to school, you'll change into these clothes at the shed. When you get to school, you'll be Sam, the new kid in the class – but Sam with a difference.'

'Sam, as in Samantha,' said Jake.

The American stood up slowly. 'You want me to be some kind of daisy? I always knew you guys were wigged out,' he said quietly. 'But this – man, this is just sick.'

'Your choice,' said Tyrone casually. 'All you have to do is be a girl for five days at school. If you agree to do that, you're in. You're one of us.'

'But...I'm Sam Lopez.' He laughed as if some dreadful misunderstanding had taken place. 'Sam Lopez does not, excuse me, go around in a girl's clothes – not for no one, no how. No way.'

'Fine.' Jake kneeled down, picked up the clothes and put them back in the bag. 'You had your chance. We had heard that Sam Lopez had the nerve to do anything. I guess we must have been misinformed.'

'Listen, you guys, be reasonable. Would any of you agree to pull this kind of stunt?'

'Nope.' I smiled. 'But then again we don't have to.'

Sam pondered for a moment. Then, muttering, 'Forget it, you freaks,' he walked quickly to the door. We heard him stomping up the stairs and slamming the door to Tyrone's bathroom.

We looked at one another, each of us kind of embarrassed by what had happened.

'It was worth a try,' said Jake.

'Yeah, really great idea of yours, Matthew,' said Tyrone.

'To be fair, it does look a bit iffy,' said Jake. 'Getting a bloke to dress up as a girl.'

'All right,' I snapped suddenly. 'So maybe I made a mistake.'

'I hope he's not trashing the bathroom,' Tyrone muttered. 'My mother will go mad.'

It was at that moment that the door opened. It was Sam. 'Gimme the bag,' he said, with an impatient, beckoning gesture of the hand.

Jake walked over and passed him the bag.

'No promises, right?' said Sam.

'Of course,' said Jake.

'I'm just thinking about it.'

'Right,' said Jake. 'Oh, and there was something else.' He fished in his pocket and took out a coloured band. 'My sis uses one of these.'

Sam held the band between two fingers and gazed at it with a look of total, unbelieving disgust, and for a moment I thought Jake was on the way to getting his other eye blackened.

'It's for keeping your hair out of your face,' he explained.

'I know what it is, doughbrain,' said Sam. Then, to my surprise, he laughed. 'You guys have some serious issues.' And he was gone.

We waited. After a couple of minutes, we heard footsteps on the stairs. The door opened and Sam walked in. The silence in the room stretched for seconds.

'So?' said Sam eventually.

'Oh...my...God,' Jake murmured.

'That is just freaky,' said Tyrone.

'Wow,' I said.

Sam stood there, hands on hips, hair swept back in a ponytail. 'What?' he said. 'What is it?'

Something about the tough-guy voice of Sam, coming from this new person, this girl, got to us all at the same time.

It was Jake who started laughing first. 'It's ridiculous,' he gasped.

Tyrone covered his face with his hands, then took a peep between them as if not quite believing what he had seen. 'Incredible,' he said.

'What exactly are you guys talking about?' Sam asked angrily.

For some reason, the situation seemed to have made me blush. 'Sorry about this, Sam,' I said, trying to keep the smile off my face. 'But there's no getting round the fact that you are just perfect – you're one hundred per cent girl.'

With a hard, dangerous look in his eye, he ambled forward. When he reached the middle of the room, he caught a glimpse of himself in the mirror over the fireplace and turned to study his reflection.

'Yup,' he said grimly. 'I'm a babe all right.'

Tyrone

Suddenly it wasn't a joke any more. The fact was that Sam looked so good as a girl that what had seemed like a funny idea a few seconds ago had taken on a deadly seriousness.

He slumped down on the sofa and picked his nose in an aggressive, showy way, as if to reassure himself that, even dressed up as a girl and with his hair in a neat ponytail, he was still the same old Sam.

'So what's the deal then?' he asked. 'Apart from trying to make me look kind of dumb, that is.'

'We don't want to make you look dumb,' said Matthew. 'We just need to get our own back on the Bitches. Show them up. Get to know some of their sad little secrets.'

'Hey, come on, guys, all this to put one over on a bunch of chicks?'

'They're not chicks,' I muttered. 'Just because we hate them it doesn't mean we have to be sexist about it.'

'Hey, who's wearing the skirt around here?' said Sam. 'From here on, I decide what's sexist, right?'

Sitting there, playing with his ponytail, Sam seemed weirdly at ease, as if, now that he was the centre of attention, he could relax – as if, in a skirt, he was more himself. 'It'll take a bit of nerve. New school and all.'

'We'll be there to help you,' I said.

Sam thought for a moment. 'We'd be in this together, right? I've never been a girl before.'

'Of course,' said Jake. 'We're the Sheds. We're a team, equal.'

Sam hitched a leg over the arm of his chair.

'OK, count me in,' he said coolly. He scratched his thigh and there was an alarming flash of his blue Jockey shorts. 'And will you guys *stop* looking up my skirt.'

Mrs Burton

At about this point, I noticed a change in little Sam. He became less defensive and leery. The inappropriate comments became less frequent. He shared jobs with Matthew. I was pleased. I thought we had cracked it.

Matthew

Life was easier after that fateful afternoon when the four of us agreed that, when Bradbury Hill returned, there would be a new pupil in Year Eight called Samantha Lopez.

Another month remained of the holidays. Jake went on a camping holiday to France with his mother and sister. Tyrone and Sam discovered that they had a shared craze for video games. Sam asked me to take him to a game of what he still insisted on calling 'soccer' and he delivered his inevitable verdict: it was a game for wusses.

It would be an exaggeration to say that my little cousin was no longer irritating – his talent to annoy was a perfect, unbreakable thing – but the knowledge that he would be soon sacrificing his precious masculinity in what I had taken to thinking of as 'Operation Samantha' calmed him down. He no longer seemed to need to prove himself cooler, smarter and more experienced than the rest of us. He still made the occasional aggressive, smart-arse remark, but the rest of us were able to laugh it off and, as often as not, Sam ended up laughing too.

Although the shadow of his mother's death still hung over him – he would drift off now and then into a numb, blank-eyed trance when something occurred to remind him of his past – my parents and I found that we could reach him in a way that had been impossible before. Mum had taken to referring to Galaxy in her everyday conversation as if she was no longer this great unmentionable thing, and to my surprise the tactic took some of the tension out of the atmosphere at home.

In the last week of the holiday, I noticed that Sam grew quieter and spent more time in his room. He had taken possession of Chrissie Smiley's bag of clothes after our meeting. I imagined him alone in there, dressing up, preparing for his debut as a girl as if he were some kind of actor just before his first night, which, I guess, in a way he was.

I would have liked to talk things through with him, to reassure him that, although he was the one who had to wear a skirt, we were all in this together, but, since the plan had been hatched, he had hardly made reference to it.

Somewhere along the line he had seemed to have decided that Operation Samantha was going to be – a one-man – a one-girl – show.

Mr Burton

It seemed to me an appropriate gesture to take the boys out for a slap-up meal on the eve of Sam's first day at school. I selected La Trattoria La Torre, a local Italian hostelry with a decent menu and cheerful service, which Mary and I like to frequent on special occasions.

Sam, I noticed, had been somewhat reserved over the past few days – doubtless his debut at Bradbury Hill was somewhat on his mind – and Matthew seemed a bit subdued too.

So it was not the easiest of social occasions. Sam's restaurant manners, to put it mildly, left a little to be desired. La Torre, he informed us, was 'phoney'. Luigi, the manager, was 'no way Italian'. He pushed his prawn cocktail away, announcing rather more loudly than was necessary that it was 'gay'.

The Burton family smiled through it all and behaved as if this kind of talk caused us absolutely no problem.

Matthew

Sam was the biggest nightmare ever that night. I know that the guy had a lot on his mind, what with having to turn into a girl the next day and all that, but did he really have to get the whole restaurant looking at us? I swear that the way he ate his pasta was one of the most truly disgusting sights I have ever seen in my life.

Mr Burton

I elected to ignore Sam's feeding-time-at-the-zoo impression.

Halfway through the meal, Mary nodded to me. I cleared my throat and raised a glass.

'A toast,' I said, 'to Sam's first day at Bradbury Hill. And to the start of Matthew's first term of his second year.'

'Gimme a break,' muttered Sam.

Matthew stared into his pasta as if it contained the secret of the universe.

'I just wanted to say,' I continued, 'that I have been extremely impressed by the way you both have conducted yourselves over the past few weeks. The situation in which we have found ourselves has not been easy, but I think both Sam and Matthew have been absolutely brilliant. Don't you, Mary?'

'I certainly do,' said Mary.

Sam made a sucking, grunting noise without looking, and I noticed a small, dangerous frown appearing on Mary's face. My wife is a wonderful woman in many ways, but she does have something of a short fuse.

'Do you have anything to say, Sam?' she asked in a strained voice.

Sam looked up, a truly stomach-churning sight with meat and red sauce spread widely around on his cheeks. 'Nope,' he said.

'I'll drive you both to school tomorrow,' I said. 'First day of term and all that.'

For some reason, this casual remark caused the boys to stop eating. They both stared at me with what appeared to be alarm.

'That's OK, Dad,' said Matthew. 'It's only ten minutes' walk.'

'I think it would be appropriate,' said Mary.

'No,' said Matthew, with a rather surprising degree of firmness. 'You know how schools are. It's better if I take him in on his first day.'

'Maybe Sam should decide that,' I said firmly.

We all looked towards Sam, who seemed actually to be burrowing into his spaghetti.

'Sam?' said Mary.

He looked up slowly, chewing, open-mouthed. When he had finished, he wiped his mouth with the back of his hand, then, noticing a couple of bits of meat on his knuckle, he frowned, then licked them off.

'Walk,' he said finally.

Jake

Matthew sent me a message later that night. It read 'OFFICIAL SAM NOW BOY2GIRL.'

5

Matthew

It was the moment of truth. The next morning, with Sam in the new uniform my mother had bought him, we set off a few minutes earlier than usual, saying goodbye to my parents at the door as if we were just normal school kids rather than soldiers of fortune setting out on a daring mission of revenge.

We walked in the direction of school. When we reached the corner, we looked back and gave my parents one last wave. We turned out of sight. Then we doubled back to the park.

Tyrone was already at the shed. Jake, as usual, was late.

We nodded a greeting to one another. Without a word, Sam reached into the new shoulder bag my father had bought him for school and took out the plastic bag containing his change of uniform.

'Time for the new me,' he said in a matter-of-fact way, then disappeared into the gents lavatory, at the back of the shed.

Two minutes, three. Jake arrived, his shirt hanging out, his hair a mess.

'Overslept,' he said. 'Where's Sam?'

Tyrone nodded in the direction of the locked door. 'Changing into a girl,' he said.

I glanced at my watch. We had eight minutes to make the ten-minute walk to Bradbury Hill. 'We've got to go,' I called out, as casually as I could manage.

'All right,' Sam snapped. 'I'm fixing my hair, OK?' Jake sighed. 'Women,' he muttered.

The lock drew back and Sam emerged, stuffing his old clothes into the plastic bag. 'Let's go,' he said.

Jake stood in front of him. 'Final check-up,' he said.

We gathered in a semicircle, inspecting the new Sam. My first impression, frankly, was that he was a bit of a disappointment. Back in the sitting room, when he had made his debut in a skirt, he had looked the real thing. Now he was more like a boy in clumsy disguise. His hair was tangled. The skirt looked a bit long. Worst of all, the white shirt seemed to be billowing outwards like a sheet in the wind.

'Isn't there anything you can do about that?' I tugged at the shirt. 'Like, tuck it in at the back?'

'It's way too big,' Sam said. 'What was it with your sister, Jake?'

Jake looked embarrassed. 'She was kind of well-developed for her age,' he said.

'Great,' Sam muttered as he tried to cram the shirt into the waist of his skirt. 'Trust you to have a sister with out-size gazungas.'

'I know what we could do,' said Tyrone. 'I'll bring a couple of pairs of socks tomorrow. You can shove them down your front.'

Sam's eyes flashed dangerously. 'You know what, fat boy, you can shove them where the sun don't shine.' He raised a warning finger, then seemed to hesitate, shifting his attention from Tyrone to something behind us.

An old woman with a small dog on a lead was standing on the path, looking at us, an expression of busybody concern on her face.

Miss Wheeler-Carrington

I remember the days when this park was nice. No litter, no dogs roaming like wolves, no swearing. It was a pleasure to come here.

Some people think that one shouldn't worry about such things as bad behaviour and nasty language, but I'm afraid that I'm a bit old-fashioned about that sort of thing.

That morning, when I saw this young girl, surrounded by boys, clearly frightened and pale-faced and angry, it made my blood boil. I knew I couldn't just walk by. It's not in my nature.

Jake

The old biddy stood there, with this terrier, both of them looking at us really defensively, as if we were criminals or something.

'Are you all right, love?' she called out.

We looked at one another, confused.

'Excuse me?' said Matthew.

'I'm not talking to you boys,' she snapped. Craning her neck like some kind of bird, she looked beyond us to where Sam was standing. 'Are these boys bothering you, dear?' she asked.

It took a moment for Sam to understand. Then he smiled. 'Nah,' he said.

'That's all right then,' said the woman. Darting one more hostile look at us, she walked on. Trouble was, Sam, being Sam, couldn't leave it there.

'Lady, I could whop their sorry asses any time,' he called out.

The woman glanced back, startled, then scurried on, tugging her little dog behind her.

Matthew

Sam was swaggering ahead of us, hands in pockets, skirt swishing aggressively, like no girl ever did, or ever will.

We followed, each of us with the same thought in our mind. Since no one else was going to say anything, I decided that it was down to me to have a word with Miss Samantha.

'Hey, Sam,' I hit a casual, this-just-occurred-to-me tone. 'Maybe it would be a good idea if you kind of acted the part too.'

Sam started whistling through his teeth – another

thing I had never heard a girl do.

I tried again. 'I mean, for instance, you didn't exactly behave like a normal girl back there when you talked to that woman.'

Sam laughed and kicked a tin can that was on the pavement into the road.

'That's because I'm not a normal girl, doofus,' he said.

'The thing is, Sam, if you don't go with this thing, we're all going to be in deep trouble,' said Tyrone. 'There's no point in dressing up female and acting more male than ever.'

'It was your plan, guys,' said Sam. 'It's kind of late to be wimping out.'

'It's not that,' I said. 'It's just that, if this is going to work, you're going to have to be a bit...I hesitated, groping in my mind for the right word. 'A bit...girly.'

Sam stopped and turned to face us, chewing all the while. 'I agreed to wear a skirt, right?' he said quietly. 'Nobody said nothing about acting girly.'

Before any of us could reply, he was walking on. 'This is just the way we modern girls are,' he called out. He jabbed the air in front of him, as if punching some invisible enemy out of the way. 'If you can't hack it, that's your problem.'

Charley

On the way to school that first day of the new term, we made a big decision. No, actually, check that – it wasn't a big decision. It was pretty small.

'I've been thinking,' Zia said suddenly. 'I think I'm through with the Sheds.'

'Tell me something new,' said Elena. 'We're all through with the Sheds.'

'I mean, I'm not going to give them a hard time any more. It's my good resolution for the term. Those boys have suffered enough.'

'Diddums,' said Elena.

As it happened, I had been thinking the same thing. The whole Burger Bill, police thing had made me feel bad.

'I'm with you, Zed,' I chipped in. 'I heard that poor old Tyrone got grounded for a week.'

'You don't mess with the Bitches,' Elena muttered.

'Think about it, the Bitches versus the Sheds,' said Zia. 'How sad is that?'

Elena looked at us. 'OK, we'll just ignore them,' she said. 'Let them get on with their miserable little lives.'

'Or,' said Zia patiently. 'We could actually apologise – draw a line under the whole thing.'

'Cool with me,' I said.

'No way.' Elena shook her head decisively.

Zia and I glanced at one another and said nothing. The fact is, El was never quite as tough as she liked to pretend.

After no more than thirty seconds, she shrugged moodily. 'Whatever. Maybe it's time for a new chapter.'

She walked ahead of us with the air of someone who had sorted out a problem all on her own.

Matthew

We were a couple of minutes late. The playground was already empty. We ran to the school hall and pushed the door. Everyone was in place, awaiting the arrival of Mrs Cartwright, the head teacher, and her staff. As the four of us made the long walk up the centre aisle to the remaining free seats in the front row, I was aware of a rustle of interest on each side. I glanced to my left to see Sam smiling this way and that, as if he were some kind of royalty.

There was no doubt about it – far from being embarrassed about the whole cross-dressing thing, he was enjoying his moment as the centre of attention.

Elena

I noticed Matthew walking between the rows of seats. I was just about to make some comment about how typical it was that they'd be late when I remembered that the boys formerly known as the Sheds were meant to be friends, so I kept shtum.

Then I saw this blonde girl striding ahead of them, cool as you like. My only thought then was – and *who* is she?

Zia

Notice her? How could anyone miss her? She walked through that hall as if she owned it.

Charley

She was chewing gum. That was the first thing I noticed. Bradbury Hill isn't the strictest place, but there's this big no-gum rule that all the teachers enforce as if sticks of gum were drugs or something. And here was this new kid, chewing away in assembly, on the first day of term.

You've got to admit, that's attitude.

Gary Laird

I didn't see her. I was probably asleep at the time.

Mark Kramer

She was a babe. All the guys looked, and most of them were thinking pretty much the same thing. Well now, what do we have here?

Matthew

We took our seats, Sam slumping down beside me with all the feminine poise of a boxer taking a break between rounds.

The teachers trooped in and took up their places on a double rank of chairs at the back of the stage and, moments later, Mrs Cartwright – better known as the 'Carthorse' – made her appearance.

When you first see the head teacher, it's not the jet-black dyed hair, the broad shoulders or the brisk, quick-paced walk that you notice but the big, saintly smile on her face. Someone at teaching school must have told her that the best way to deal with kids is to grin your way out of trouble at all times, because Mrs Cartwright goes about her daily life at school with the goofy, happy air of someone who has some wonderful news that she just longs to tell you.

The effect, when she is dealing with what she likes to call 'inappropriate behaviour' is weirdly scary because, the deeper trouble you are in, the wider the smile on her face. As if playing up to her reputation as a grinning psycho, the head allows herself now and then to blow her stack, raging at the entire school in assembly when a particular bout of inappropriateness looks as if it might get out of hand. It is rumoured that, when the stress of school life becomes too much for her, she steps into a store cupboard in her office, closes the door behind her and screams her head off for a couple of minutes before emerging, calmer and with the famous smile back on her face.

So the Carthorse launched into her start-of-the-year speech. There was a bit of chat about the holiday, some guff about the school play that was due at the end of term. She introduced a couple of new teachers, a woman in her twenties and a porky, middle-aged guy who was taking over the first year. Then she did something rather unexpected and scary.

After she had introduced the new teachers, she gave us a big, all-inclusive grin and said, 'There is someone else I would also very much like to mention at this point. A significant new arrival in Year Eight.'

Uh-oh.

To my left, Tyrone groaned quietly.

'He's joining us from his school on the west coast of America,' the head was saying. 'I'm sure you'll all go out of your way to make him feel very welcome.'

I tried to swallow, but I found that my mouth was dry.

'Sam Lopez.' Mrs Cartwright peered into the audience, shielding her eyes with her hand like someone scanning the horizon. 'Where is he?'

For a few seconds there was a restless stirring in the ranks as everyone looked around them for the new boy.

Then slowly, coolly brushing something from his skirt, Sam took to his feet.

'I'm here, ma'am,' he said.

Zia

We laughed. That first assembly is always a rather tense occasion and, when this Sam character turned out to be a girl, it broke the atmosphere. It's good when something happens which makes a teacher look a bit stupid and, if that teacher happens to be Mrs Cartwright and she's standing up in front of the whole school doing her Hitler-at-a-youth-rally act, it's very good indeed.

The American girl looked round at us and grinned, which made us laugh even more. It took several seconds for the head to restore order.

Matthew

Mrs Cartwright's smile became even more fixed and phoney than usual.

'I was under the impression that Sam Lopez was a boy,' she said.

'Not this Sam Lopez, she ain't,' said Sam, and there was more laughter in the hall.

'You're Sam Lopez, as in Samantha?' she asked.

'Nope.' Sam kept to his feet, now clearly enjoying the moment. 'I am Sam, ma'am. Sam is what my mom called me.'

'She, christened you Sam?'

'She was a feminist, ma'am.'

The mention of Sam's late mother, or maybe the reference to feminism, seemed to fluster Mrs Cartwright. 'Ah good, interesting – well, that's the first surprise of the term.' She laughed in a tinkling, fake way. 'Now that we've discovered exactly what sex you are, Bradbury Hill welcomes you, Sam Lopez.'

'Thank you, ma'am.' Sam sat down slowly.

Fifteen minutes into the new term and he had already made his mark.

Mrs Cartwright

It is an important occasion, that first assembly, and frankly I was not best pleased that an administrative error had caused a distraction. As I explained to Steve Forrester later, the fault was not entirely mine. Mrs Burton had called me during the holiday. I was not what I call switched on. The American child had moved schools so often that there were no records of his – of her – past education.

It seemed to me that Mrs Burton had been referring to a boy, but I assumed I had mistaken 'he' for 'she'. There had been no reason not to assume that Sam was short for Samuel.

As for the child herself, I was vaguely aware that she was showing rather less respect than I would have liked but then, to be fair, this incident of gender confusion had been unusually public. I assumed that her apparent chippiness was a cover-up. Sam was a shy thirteen-year-old girl. I honestly believed that.

Elena

Normally I don't like show-offs, but there was something about the new girl that made me want to get to know her. The way she went, 'I am Sam, ma'am,' when she said her mum was a feminist, like she was shocked that she had to explain it. I suppose it was just that she acted like most of us would like to act in that situation.

It should have been her that was made to look stupid. Instead it was old Carthorse. I was, 'Hey, I could get to like this girl.'

Matthew

Sam was flirting with danger. Every kid in the hall knew that – every kid, that is, except for Sam Lopez. And it wasn't the head teacher that was the problem.

Gary

I woke up in the middle of assembly and there was this brat, this new brat, behaving like she was totally it. Who did this skinny little ponytailed dork think she was exactly? It was time for her first lesson in the facts of life at Bradbury Hill.

Matthew

We were among the last of those emerging from the school hall after the head had finished her speech. Sam walked beside us, now and then smiling at those who stared at him.

'Stick close to us,' Jake murmured, but Sam was having too good a time to pay any attention. As we crossed the playground, the unavoidable, muscular presence of Gary Laird loomed up between us.

It would be wrong to say that Gary hung out with a rough crew. He was a one-man rough crew. He hung out with nobody because he liked nobody and nobody liked him. Six foot and big with it, with cropped dark hair, he was like a cartoon version of teenage yobbery. When it came to spreading fear, Gary was top of Year Ten, unrivalled by lesser, smaller thugs. Others bullied out of fun or boredom – for Gary, it was a career, it was a vocation.

'Hey, Yank chick,' he called out.

Sam kept walking. Gary strode beside him across the playground, a towering, mighty figure.

'Want a date, Yank chick?' Gary taunted.

Sam stopped walking. 'What exactly is your problem?' he asked, his eyes narrowing dangerously.

'I've heard all about American girls.' Gary chuckled nastily.

'Easy, Gary,' said Tyrone. 'She's new.'

Gary ignored him. 'Everyone knows about Yank girls.'

'What do they know?' Sam asked.

Either the question was too difficult for Gary's apology of a brain to process or something in Sam's manner gave him pause. He changed his line of attack.

'Are you chewing gum, Yank chick?' he said in a low voice.

'Yup,' said Sam.

'I don't like people chewing in my face. It's not respectful, see.'

Sam chewed more openly. 'Go blow smoke up it, loser.'

Gary made a sudden movement of his right hand but Sam hardly blinked. Jake and Tyrone closed in but, at that moment, someone else intervened.

Charley

'Leave her alone, Gary,' I said.

Slowly, he turned his horrible face in my direction, narrowing his eyes as if my words were slowly sinking into his brain like ink into blotting paper. I was aware of Zia and Elena on each side of me. It was an awkward moment – no one in their right mind, female or male, gets on the wrong side of Gary Laird – but at least the three of us were in this together.

'What's this – girl power?' he snarled.

'No, it's just—' I was about to say something reasonable and non-hostile about joining the human race or picking on someone his own size or violence solving nothing, when this Sam character spoke up.

'That's right, doughbrain,' she said, eyeballing Gary like she was about to hit him, rather than the other way round.

'It's girl power. Girls together.' She poked him in the chest with a finger. 'Deal with it.'

Wow. Gary seemed actually to swell up with rage. His right fist clenched and—

'Any danger of you people honouring me with your presence?' Steve Forrester stood at the top of the steps.

Gary shuffled off, knuckles dragging on the ground, muttering revenge, and Sam made her way towards us. 'Hey, thanks for that,' she said, smiling at each of us.

'No problem,' said Elena. 'Girl power, right?'

And Sam laughed as if this was the best joke ever cracked. 'Yeah, right,' she said.

Gary

She got lucky. Next time she was toast. She was a dead
girl walking. End of story.

6

Matthew

A word about Steve – not Mr Forrester, mind, not sir; but Steve.

He was cooler than any teacher had a right to be.

He liked the right music. He understood jokes. He watched the right TV programmes. He was kind of good looking in an overgrown schoolboy sort of way and had played tennis for the county. He was the only teacher in the history of education who could wear jeans without looking a prat. If the government wanted to run an advertising campaign to show just how great working as a teacher could be, Steve would be their man.

The Shed Gang had seen right through Steve Forrester. We clocked early on, when he was our English teacher in the first year, that he was just too nice to be genuine, too obviously normal to be a teacher. He must have sensed that we weren't taken in by him because sometimes, when he talked to us, I noticed the faintest flicker of disdain cross his face. One of the girls – Zia, it was – picked up on this and played along with it. By the end of the year, the three of them were firmly in place as the aristocrats of the class during English lessons, while Jake, Tyrone and me were down among the dead men.

It would not be true to say that Steve actively disliked boys, more that he preferred girls, found them easier to talk to and understand – which, of course, was excellent news for little Miss Lopez.

That first morning, as the Shed Gang claimed its usual position at the back of the class, I watched Steve as he chatted to Sam, who was seated between Elena and Charley. It was clear from the teacher's expression that he already approved of the new girl. She may have looked slender and vulnerable, yet she had stood up for herself, made her mark, in assembly. She was the sort of person he could relate to, that he enjoyed teaching. She had, to use one of his favourite words, 'character'.

Steve Forrester

There had been a situation assembly. The new year had not started as smoothly as one would have hoped. Already there had been a hint of trouble outside class – inevitably involving the appalling Gary Laird. I knew from experience that we would be sailing on choppy waters through that first lesson, and beyond.

One way of dealing with this kind of potential problem is to ignore it, to pretend that all is normal. Personally, I prefer a more direct and honest approach.

The new girl, Sam Lopez, had upset the inbuilt interpersonal dynamic within Year Eight. I was glad to see that within an hour of being at Bradbury Hill, she had distanced herself from her cousin, Matthew Burton, and his friends – an unhelpful influence, in my experience – and aligned herself with Charley, Zia and Elena. The four of them occupied a table near the front of the classroom while the Matthew trio skulked at the back, as is their habit.

But no one is going to settle down until the new girl had been assimilated into the herd. A certain amount of sniffing round each other's bottoms (I am speaking figuratively here) needed to occur, so that morning I suggested that we all got to know one another. I said that being in Year Eight was different. We were all changing. It was a good moment to make a new start. Some of us – I may have darted a quick glance to the back of the class – could do with a new start.

I invited each of the class to stand up and, for a moment or two, tell the rest of us what had happened to them during the holidays.

Tyrone

It was a typical bit of Steve touchy-feeliness – sometimes he's that close to being a hippy.

Elena stood up to tell us how she had learned to surf in Cornwall. A girl called Julie followed her. Julie hadn't been away at all, as per usual, so she had just messed around. Dave had been given a dog. Kofi had been mugged for his phone. It was all pretty much the usual stuff.

Until Steve wandered over to a table near the front and, with a special you're among friends smile, said, 'Your turn, Sam. How have your holidays been?'

Steve Forrester

The American girl stood up and faced the class.

'Well,' she said. 'First of all, my mom died, which kind of sucked.' She looked around, paused, then broke the silence with a casual, 'But you know what they say. Shit happens.'

All eyes turned towards me. I may have a relaxed style, but it's well known that I take a firm line on language. On this occasion, though, I judged it prudent to give Sam Lopez the benefit of the doubt. It was a tough moment for her. We could go over the rules about swearing later.

'So I left my home,' Sam continued. 'Said goodbye to my town, to my posse and to the whole good ole US of A and came over to stay with my cousin, Matthew Burton.'

Heads turned towards Matthew, who raised a hand in acknowledgement.

'Since then, there's been good stuff and bad stuff,' said Sam. 'I got me some new clothes. Several times I nearly got run down on account of the weird side of the road you people drive on. I hung out with Matthew and his' – she gave an odd little smile – 'gang.'

'Bad luck,' said Charley, just loud enough to hear.

'Thank you, Charley,' I said.

'That's about it,' said Sam.

'You've had quite a summer, Sam.' I smiled down at her. 'We all hope you'll be very happy at Bradbury Hill.'

'Yeah, cool.' Sam sat down.

We went on with the session. At one point, Jake – inevitably – tried it on, saying he had been involved in a bit of trouble at a burger bar, but then he grinned in that peculiar, irritating way of his and said, 'You know what they say, shit happens.'

So then we had the swearing discussion. Jake protested that I hadn't said anything when Sam had sworn. There was a free and frank discussion in which I pointed out that any more swear words from anyone, including Sam, would result in a detention.

As I said this – I'm pretty sure I'm right here – the new girl looked up at me and winked.

I had the brief, alarming suspicion that she had somehow set the whole thing up.

Matthew

Something strange happened during that lesson. We sat at the back, the Sheds, tense at first, worried that Sam was going to crack – say or do something that was so obviously make-believe that Operation Samantha would be exposed, leaving the three of us in the deepest doo-doo in the history of deep doo-doos.

But, as the lesson went on, and Sam did his Little-Orphan-Annie speech, it became clear that he was a natural actor and now he was getting into character.

Another thing. What had been so irritating about him when he was a boy – his confidence, his drawling accent, his need to show off and shock people and generally draw attention to himself – seemed almost charming now that he was a girl. Starting out at a new school in a new country should have been tough, but Sam, the female Sam, was making it look easy. Already, he was Year Eight's new cutie.

'I think this might just work,' I murmured to Jake as Sam talked on.

Jake shook his head. 'Not when he's flashing that boy's watch, it won't.'

Ah. I looked closer. On Sam's wrist, occasionally showing under the sleeve of his jacket, was a watch that was straight from his male past – flashy, big and sporty.

At the end of the lesson, we were due to take a twenty-minute break. As Sam approached, chatting to Zia, I tried to attract his attention but, almost as if he had forgotten who I was, he walked straight past me.

In the playground, when the two of them had been joined by Charley and Elena, I tried again.

'Everything OK, Sam?' I asked.

The four of them looked at me coolly as if my interruption was profoundly unwelcome.

'Sure,' Sam said. 'Why shouldn't it be?'

'I just thought I'd watch out for you.' I glanced in the direction of his wrist. 'I wanted to watch how you were getting on. I didn't want you to lose it.'

'What's he talking about?' Sam asked the girls.

'I think he's trying to get you to look at your wristwatch,' said Charley.

Sam flicked his wrist, carelessly revealing the evidence. 'Hey, you're wearing a boy's watch,' said Elena.

'I lent her mine,' I said quickly. 'I...I didn't want her to be late for lessons on her first day at school.'

'What you talkin' about?' Sam laughed. 'This is my watch. In the States, all the girls are wearing sports watches. It's the hot new fashion statement.'

'Really?' Elena, who lives to accessorise, took Sam's wrist and looked more closely at the watch.

I stammered something about the watch looking rather like mine, but no one was listening to me. As the three girls fussed over Sam's left wrist, he looked over their heads in my direction, smiled happily, then jerked his head in an eloquent gesture of dismissal.

I walked across the playground to where Jake and Tyrone were standing.

'How's she doing?' Jake asked.

He glanced back at the group of girls. Zia was actually touching Sam's blond hair admiringly. The four of them made a picture of girly togetherness.

'She's doing great,' I said.

Tyrone

Face it, we took our eye off the ball. We were so hung up on how Sam had managed to get in with Elena's crew within, like, seconds of arriving at Bradbury Hill that we forgot one crucial fact.

The guy was trouble – always had been, always would be. Even at that moment when it looked like he was the

Miss American Pie of Year Eight, some kind of bother would be heading his way like a heat-seeking missile.

Gary Laird has a brain the size of a small, dried pea – getting to the end of the simplest thought is sometimes beyond him – but, like an elephant, he has a memory. If someone has annoyed him in even the slightest way, that person will be added to Gary's private shopping list, the one headed 'People I Must Hurt Very Badly Today'.

Right now, Sam was top of that list. Gary had seen the American girl making herself the centre of attention in assembly. He had sensed a weird lack of respect or fear when he had spoken to her in the playground. All through the first lesson of term, that small, dried pea of his was filled with thoughts of violent revenge.

Jim Kiley

I didn't want to get involved. Keep your nose clean, that's me. But have you seen Gary? Have you met him? He's not the sort of person you say 'no' to – not if you fancy keeping your looks, that is. So when Gary asked me to get the new girl to the science block, I wasn't about to ask any questions. I guessed that he wasn't exactly planning to talk sweet nothings to her but I was like, hey, not my problem. That's the way it is at Bradbury Hill – at least when Gary Laird's around.

Gary

It was my moment. I'd been thinking about it all through the lesson. I was focused, ready. I felt very, very good.

Elena

Sam was telling us all this crazy stuff about her life in America when Jim Kiley, one of those nervous, invisible types from Year Ten, came up and told her that Mr Smart, the deputy head, needed to see her for registration in the science block.

It was only after she was making her way across the playground that we began to be suspicious.

Mr Smart in the science block? He taught geography. And why should Sam need to register right now? If it was some kind of joke or set-up, then it wasn't exactly subtle.

'Gary!' It was Charley who got there first. 'It's a trap.' Sam had turned the corner. The three of us started walking after her.

It was at that precise moment that this sound – a yodelling, deafening bellow – echoed around the playground. It was coming from the science block.

Zia

For a few seconds there was this 'What the—?' moment in the playground. Then everyone began to move in the direction of the noise.

When we turned the corner, there was already a crowd of people gathered near the entrance to the science block. We pushed our way to the front.

There a weird and amazing sight greeted our eyes. Gary Laird was bent double. His face, flushed a dark red, was at a painful angle to his neck, and from his gaping mouth there came an agonised lowing sound, like a cow giving birth. Standing over him, looking, if anything, smaller than usual, was Sam. She was holding Gary's left ear in her hand, stretching it away from his Neanderthal skull.

It was astonishing, unnatural – funny but also scary – to see the Terror of Year Ten so completely and humiliatingly at the mercy of this small, blonde girl.

'It's the American kid,' someone said.

'Go for it, girl,' someone else shouted to nervous, excited laughter.

Sam ignored us all and concentrated on her victim. 'You wanted something, buddy-boy?' She spoke in a voice of cold, controlled rage. 'Was there something you had to say to me?'

'Nooo,' Gary moaned. 'Nothing.'

Sam gave the ear such a savage tug that the boy in front of me winced and looked away.

'Don't get me mad now,' Sam said through clenched teeth. 'I just know you wanted to say something.'

'Ssss.' A noise like a punctured tyre came from Gary. 'Ssssorry!'

Sam jerked the ear again. 'Sorry, Sam,' she said.

'Sorry, Sam.'

It was at this moment of surrender that someone at the back of the crowd shouted, 'It's Forrester.'

As Steve Forrester pushed his way forward, Sam glanced up and seemed for a moment about to let Gary go. She released the ear but, at the very moment that her victim relaxed, she let fly with her right foot, catching him with a vicious force between the legs. Gary seemed actually to lift off the ground before landing on the tarmac, a hunched, quivery hulk of agony.

'What's going on?' Steve asked.

Sam tucked a lock of blonde hair behind her ear and widened her eyes innocently. 'I was attacked, sir.' The voice was suddenly small and timid. 'Someone told me the deputy head wanted to see me. Then, when I came around the corner, this guy jumped me.' She briefly seemed to be about to cry. 'For no reason, sir.'

Steve looked down to where Gary was still writhing in agony, both hands between his legs. 'Is this true, Gary?' he asked.

Gary was having difficulty breathing. 'She's a... psycho,' he groaned.

'Oh, yeah, and I suppose she attacked you,' one of the girls called out from the crowd.

'I saw what happened,' someone else said. 'Sam was just walking along, minding her own business, when he grabbed her.'

Gary heaved himself so that he was sitting on the tarmac. 'I just wanted a quiet word,' he said sulkily. 'There was no need for' – he rubbed his left ear – 'all that.'

Steve Forrester laughed coldly. 'It sounds to me that at last you've met someone who can stand up for herself,' he said.

Gary tried to say something, but Steve had clearly made up his mind. 'I'll be reporting this to Mrs Cartwright,' he said.

'As for you, Miss Lopez...' He turned to Sam, who was tucking her shirt into her skirt. 'You've got to learn that violence solves absolutely nothing in this life. And kicking a boy where you did can be very painful for him. D'you understand?'

Sam nodded. 'Yes, sir,' she said quietly.

'All right then. Go and tidy yourself up before the next lesson.'

The crowd parted as Sam made her way towards the main entrance, the victorious gladiator, the little girl bullfighter who had slain a mighty beast. There were mutters of congratulation. 'Way to go, supergirl,' someone shouted.

We watched her go, saw her push her way through the doors and into the toilets.

The boys' toilets.

Elena

We were like, *Huh?* Then we saw Matt Burton making his way to the toilets too.

Matthew

He had blown it. We were convinced about that. First of all, he had made Gary Laird beg for mercy – something which no one, boy or girl, had ever managed to do. Then, as if that wasn't bad enough, he had barged into the boys' toilets, watched by half the school.

Trying to look casual, I followed him in. Sam was at the urinal, casually hitching up his skirt.

'What are you doing?' I hissed.

'What does it look like?'

'But you're a girl.'

He glanced down and made a strange, snickering sound. 'I don't think so.'

'You know what I mean. Operation Samantha.'

He finished peeing, then ambled over to the mirror. 'Oh, yeah,' he said, tugging his hairband off and shaking his hair out. 'I'm a babe. It clean slipped my mind.'

He looked at me. My panic must have been obvious because he shrugged, almost apologetically, and muttered, 'I was kind of preoccupied with mashing that guy's face.'

I glanced towards the door. Any moment someone would come in.

'Get your hairband on,' I said. 'Leave this to me.'

He gathered his hair and slipped the band over his head in a way which I have to admit was surprisingly expert.

'Don't get the wrong idea.' I put an arm around his shoulders.

He jumped away as if I had an electric current running through my right arm. 'What you doing, you freak?' he said.

'Getting you out of a mess.' I stepped forward and put an arm around him again. 'This won't take long,' I said. 'Just act upset.'

I opened the door. Elena, Zia and Charley were waiting in the corridor outside.

'Come on, Sam,' I said in a gentle, nurse-like voice. 'It's all right. The girls will look after you now.'

Sam's head was lowered. I felt him relax beneath my arm. The cute, vulnerable, female Sam was there once more.

'What...what happened?' he murmured in a stunned voice.

'You went into the wrong toilet, didn't you?' I smiled at the girls. 'She's in shock.'

'But...' Sam looked around wonderingly. 'In the States, the guys and the girls share toilets. I never knew... God, I'm so embarrassed.'

Personally, I thought this was pushing it a bit, but the girls fell for it big time.

'Oh, poor Sam.' Elena stepped forward, arms out-stretched. Sam allowed himself to be embraced.

After a few moments of sisterly cuddling, he was ushered away by the girls, who were making comforting, cooing noises.

As I watched them go, Sam flicked me the finger behind his back.

I allowed myself a little smile.

Gary

She caught me off guard. For a girl, she was surprisingly. strong. Mean with it too. I only wanted to teach her some manners, but at the end of the day it was me who had a throbbing ear and an appointment to see the head. She was trouble, that Sam Lopez. I could have sorted her out, no problem, but after that day I decided I had better things to do.

7

Charley

A whole sisterhood, we-are-family thing was kicking in. It had been quite a day for Sam. She had stood up to the Carthorse. She had talked about her mum in class. She had been attacked by Gary Laird. She had visited a boy's lavatory by mistake.

Now she was in need of some good old girl talk.

That lunchtime, we were in early to grab our usual corner table in the dining room. Sam was still looking a bit pale and shaken from what had happened, so we just stepped on the gas-pedal and chatted away. There was no doubt that she was one of us now. As far as we were concerned, she was a Bitch through and through.

Matthew

We were late for lunch and ended up on the big table with a load of Year Sevens. I noticed that Sam was sitting with the girls over in the corner, not saying much but just kind of listening while major-league girl talk was going on all around him.

I didn't envy him, to tell the truth. All that chatting and yapping is pretty alien to a guy. We can communicate well enough with a few words, grunts and facial expressions, but they seem to feel the need to verbalise just about everything and anything. It seems that, as soon as a thought comes into their heads (sometimes even before a thought comes into their heads) they have to share it with others.

If I were a sexist (which, thank goodness, I'm not), I might say that this makes them more superficial than us.

I tried to catch Sam's eye, but whatever they were talking about was certainly occupying his attention.

Elena

The great thing about us is that we can say anything. There are no boundaries, no whoops-I'd-better-keep-quiet-about-that, when the three of us are together. Sooner or later, everything – even total blush-making stuff about Mark Kramer, The Date That Never Was – comes out. I guess it must be different in the States, because Sam just looked from one of us to another, jaw gently sagging.

Charley

Here's me at lunch that day: 'You know what I almost said when Steve asked us what happened to us in the holidays?'

'About Elena falling for Mark Kramer?' Zia asked innocently.

'Actually, I was going to say, "Well, Steve, my big news this summer was that I started."'

'Oh, yesss!' Elena clapped so loudly that the people at the next table glanced in our direction.

'Cramps and everything,' I said, allowing a hint of pride to enter my voice.

'Good old Charley,' said Zia. 'Put up the flags.'

'The red flags,' said Elena, laughing.

I noticed that Sam was looking a bit confused, so, dropping my voice, I told her that I had been a bit worried last year on account of virtually every girl in our year having started except me. I was kind of relieved. My mum actually came over all teary when I told her: 'My little girl's a woman,' she sobbed. A tad embarrassing but sort of sweet.

Sam still had this vacant look on her face. 'Er, started?' she said.

'You know, the curse,' said Elena.

'She's come on,' said Zia.

'The old red devils,' I said. 'I've got the painters in.'

By now Sam was looking really confused. 'Excuse me?' she said.

I put a hand on her arm and murmured, 'Period, Sam: got my period.'

'Ah...right.' Sam nodded slowly as if she didn't know what to say. I thought maybe we should change the subject but, as is her habit, Elena managed to crank up the embarrassment quotient. She may look like cherry pie, but she has the tact and delicacy of a charging bison, that girl.

Elena

I'm like, 'Duh. You *must* have known what we were talking about.'

'Maybe it's some kind of British thing,' Sam said.

'Menstruation,' murmured Zia.

'Of course,' said Sam, kind of unconvincingly.

'When did you start, Sam?' I asked, trying to put her at her ease.

'Me? Erm...I'm kinda still waiting.'

We must have looked a bit surprised because Sam goes, 'I guess it's because my mom never gave me cereal for breakfast. I've always been kind of irregular, if you know what I mean.'

There was a long, long silence of about three seconds. Then I said, in my kindest voice, 'It's not like going to the loo, Sam. It's...different.'

Sam seemed embarrassed. 'Sure, I know that,' she said. 'I'm totally cool with the old cramps and stuff.'

Charley was giving me her usual shut-up-Elena look, but I decided it was best to be completely open with Sam. 'We won't tell the others,' I said. 'Some of the girls can get a bit mean if they know you're a bit retarded in that department – particularly since you're kind of flat-chested too.'

Sam looked down at the totally boob-free zone that was her chest. 'Getting kind of personal here, aren't we?' She muttered.

'Yeah, give it a break, El,' said Zia.

'I'm only telling Sam because I had that problem myself,' I explained reasonably.

It was at that moment that I had a rather brilliant idea. 'In fact,' I said. 'I might be able to help you.'

Mrs Burton

It was my decision not to tell Sam about the slightly changed circumstances of our situation. Jeb Durkowitz, the attorney in San Diego with whom I had dealt following my sister's death, had telephoned us some three weeks before the new term started.

It turned out that Gail had not been as completely hopeless when it came to practical matters as we had assumed. She had left a will in her bank vault. A lot of it was nonsense – New Age stuff about the need for Sam to be rebirthed on the eighteenth summer solstice and so on – but in its last paragraph my little sister had decreed that half of her estate should be kept in trust for Sam while the other half should go to his carer to cover the cost of his upbringing.

This was hardly relevant, I pointed out to Mr Durkowitz, since Gail's estate consisted of a tepee, a few mystic beads and the car that was destroyed in the crash that killed her.

'Actually not,' said the lawyer. 'Your sister was rather wealthier than even she knew.'

And in flat, lawyerly tones, he revealed the bizarre truth. Tod Strange, the pop musician of the group 666, to whom Gail had been briefly married, had died from a drug-related 'accident' six months before Gail's death. He had no family and the court decided that his musical royalties should pass directly to his ex-wife.

'Heavy metal turns out to be somewhat profitable,' Mr Durkowitz continued.

He was right. Two million dollars was now added to Gail's estate. We needed to set up a trust for Sam. The other million was for us to spend on his upbringing.

I needed to sit down.

There was more. 'The 666 back catalogue is a big seller,' said the lawyer. 'Royalties are currently running at around three quarters of a million dollars every year.'

'Good old 666,' I said faintly.

'There was one other thing,' said Mr Durkowitz. 'Nothing for you to worry about, but, while looking into all this, I discovered that Sam's biological father, Anthony Lopez, has recently been released from jail. He has no claims on either Sam or on the money, but I thought that it was only right that you should be aware of the situation.'

Mr Burton

Mary and I talked it over until well after eleven o'clock that night and finally decided that we should wait a while before breaking the news to Sam.

It was a tricky call. On the one hand, Sam had every right to know that, thanks to his mother and the late Mr Tod Strange, he was now a wealthy boy. On the other, life was confusing enough for him right now and he had his new school to deal with.

We didn't think any more about Mr Lopez. He had shown no interest in his boy in the past so why should he now?

Crash Lopez

I'm an instinctive, live-for-the-minute guy, but I have my habits, my routines. So when I'd spent a little time in the local penitentiary – and I've got to admit that's happened a few times down the years – I'd always do the same thing.

I'd go to a bar, buy myself a drink and ring my ex-wife, Galaxy, to check out how it's hanging with my little family. It was true that I hadn't actually seen them in person since the misunderstanding which led to my marriage going down the toilet – I had people to see, deals to do – but, no matter where I was, old Galaxy and my boy Sam were never far from my thoughts.

But this time when I rang, some stranger picked up. He said that there'd been a car crash and that Galaxy was, as he put it, 'no longer with us.'

'No longer with who?' I said.

'As in, she's gone to a better place,' said the guy. 'What you talkin' about? What better place? San Francisco? New York?'

'She's dead,' said the guy. 'There was a car crash thing on her way back from a party.'

Dead? *Dead?* I hung up, went back to the bar, bought another drink, then another. I felt sick to my stomach at the news – Galaxy may have been kind of a screwball, but she was my kind of screwball. For an ex-wife, she meant a lot to me, that girl.

And soon there were other questions spinning round and round in my head. If Galaxy was gone, where was Sam? What happened to the kid? Who's got my son?

Ottoleen Lopez

Money? What money? No way is that the reason Crash goes on this big mission to find Sam. The fact that a couple of million bucks is at the end of this particular rainbow hardly even occurred to him. He's a family guy. I respect him for that.

Charley

Let's be honest here. That whole best-pals stunt she pulled on Sam's first day was pure Elena. Much as I love her, El likes to be at the centre of things.

After the last lesson, she put on that distracted, slightly distant air that Zed and I have learned down the years can mean only one thing. El has a plan – personal, private and maybe a bit shifty. When she has to break the news of this plan, the opening move is always the same.

'Oh, by the way, I forgot to tell you.' She frowned as if suddenly remembering something. 'Sam's coming back with me.'

'Great,' said Zia. 'It's all back to El's place.'

'Hey, maybe it would be better if it was just me and her this time. We, er…we don't want to crowd her.'

'Crowd her?' I said. Elena has many talents but excuse-making is not one of them.

'Yeah, on her first day. Besides, I want to give her a present. It's kind of personal.'

'Yeah, right,' I said. 'You just want her to be more your friend than our friend.'

'Hello,' said Elena. 'Just how old are we?' With an irritating little smile, she went off to find Sam.

Matthew

We were waiting at the gate for Sam when he came out of the main building, chatting away to Elena as if they had known each other forever.

He was about to walk by us when almost as an afterthought he wandered over and said, 'I'm swinging by El's place. I'll catch ya later.'

'Couldn't you do that some other day?' I said, flashing a fake smile in the direction of Elena, who stood waiting for her new pal about ten metres away. 'My parents will really want to know how you got on on your first day.'

'I'll tell 'em later,' said Sam.

I dropped my voice. 'What about changing back? How you going to manage that?'

Sam patted his bag. 'Got the stuff here,' he said. 'Lighten up, guys.' He winked. 'It's what you wanted, isn't it? A spy in the house of the enemy.'

'Come on, Sam,' Elena called out. 'You can hear the latest Shed news later.'

'Cooomiiiing,' Sam responded in an irritatingly girly sing-song voice, and was gone.

Elena

Here's something that Elena Griffiths sussed about Sam Lopez, way before anyone else. She was shy. She may have come on like Little Miss Confident on that first day, but underneath she was quaking like a leaf in a gale.

It takes someone who understands shyness – i.e. me – to see that quite often the more you talk, the more scared you really are.

That whole period thing at lunch had tipped me off. Sam was actually blushing when Charley went on about having started. That was why I made that comment about her being a bit lacking in the boob department. I wanted to show her over here in England, we believe in sharing. We are there for each other.

'If you want to talk about your mother, that would be fine,' I said in my most sympathetic voice as we made our way home.

'That's OK, thanks,' said Sam.

'I'm a really good listener. Everybody says so.'

'I'm sure you are.' She smiled gratefully. 'But...maybe some other time.'

'Just say the word,' I said, only slightly hurt that my new friend was keeping her most important feelings to herself.

When we reached the house and went to my room, she seemed shyer than ever. I had started getting out of my school clothes when I noticed that she was just standing there, like frozen to the spot, staring out of the window, as if where she came from no one actually undressed in front of someone else.

So, to make her feel more at ease, I got into my everyday clothes and gave her the present I had been thinking about since lunch. I reached into my top drawer and there, at the back, was the item of clothing that, only twelve months ago, had meant so much to me.

'What is it?' she said, squeezing it nervously.

'It's a bra. Enhanced. Padded. It's really good until you get your own. Try it on.'

She was blushing. 'Maybe when I get home,' she said.

'No.' Firmly I started unbuttoning her shirt but she stepped back.

'OK, I'll do it,' she said.

She turned her back to me, took off her shirt and slipped the bra over her shoulders. For a few seconds, she fumbled hopelessly with the hooks. Laughing, I slapped away her hands and did it myself. 'You'd better practise this at home,' I said.

The bra was in place. Still with her back to me, she put her white school shirt on. Then she turned around slowly, her eyes closed.

'Much better,' I said.

She opened her eyes and looked down. 'Wow,' she said. 'I'm seriously stacked.'

Mr Burton

Looking back on it, I suppose that there was something rather different about the atmosphere that night. Matthew had returned alone. He always needs half an hour or so lolling about in front of the television to recover from school, but on this day he seemed moodier than usual.

Sam, on the other hand, was surprisingly chirpy when he returned about an hour later. He pronounced Bradbury Hill to be 'A-OK'. When I told him that I was preparing his favourite pasta puttanesca for supper, he said, 'Hey, neat.'

I remember thinking that 'neat' seemed an oddly un-Sam-like word.

Tyrone

My mother has never had a great sense of timing. She seems to have this perfect instinct for the worst possible moment for her to go on one of her campaigns.

Now, at the start of a new school year, with Operation Samantha going critical, she decided that a) I had put on too much weight over the summer holidays, b) I was probably well on the way to becoming a full-on criminal after the business at Burger Bill's, and c) the amount of time I was spending with Jake and Matthew almost certainly meant that I was gay.

So that night, we had one of our talks.

I can take almost anything that life has to throw at me – except my mother's talks.

She made a special supper – or at least as special as the Kirov diet, which apparently keeps all the top ballerinas as thin as grass, will allow. Then, afterwards, she sat in the sitting room. She put on her special sympathetic face and spoke in her best sympathetic voice.

'I was thinking, Ty,' she said. 'Maybe this term you should get out a little more.'

'What?'

'I think I've been a little tough on you recently.' Mum put on her loving-parent smile. Perhaps it's time for you to spread your wings a little – socially, I mean.'

I looked at her. Was this some kind of joke? Face it, I've never exactly been the wing-spreading type. 'I'm OK,' I said. 'I go out with Matthew and Jake and Sam. I'm fine.'

My mother frowned. The little vein in her temple, which throbs at times of stress, went into medium-throb mode. 'I wasn't referring to those boys,' she said. 'I meant…nice people.' She held up a hand before I could interrupt. 'I'm not criticising your friends. I'm sure they're perfectly fine. In their own way.'

'Mum,' I said. 'Why don't you just come out with what you have in mind?'

'I'm going to lunch with the Laverys on Sunday. I met them recently at a dinner – charming people. He's a lawyer. Very...distinguished.'

'Rich, you mean.'

'They are quite comfortable, as it happens, but that's not the point.' She paused, and I waited to discover where all this was leading.

'I believe they've got a daughter,' she said casually. 'Apparently, she's a bit of a loner too.'

'Mum, no.'

But my mother was smiling mistily. 'A lawyer's daughter,' she said. 'Think of it.'

Ottoleen

I'm working at a topless joint in Pasadena when me and Crash get hitched up. He comes in looking for a guy called Harry Gatz, who used to own the place when he and Crash did some business together. Crash has had a small problem with the law and has been out of the loop for a while and now he's back, looking for Harry.

But Harry's long gone. He has sold the place and headed east. These days it isn't called Dirty Harry's any more, but the Big Top.

Crash takes all this kind of badly. Earlier that day he's heard that his ex-wife has been killed in a car crash while he's inside, he doesn't even know where his kid is, and now Harry's gone too. Harry, it turns out, owes Crash big time – in fact, the way he tells it, Crash has taken the rap for the both of them.

So, like I'm saying, Crash is taking it kind of badly.

It's three in the morning. The place is dead. This little guy in a sharp suit and a tragic face has been drowning his sorrows all night. I'm bringing him his zillionth bourbon on the rocks when he looks up and says, 'What's a nice girl like you doing in a dive like this?'

OK, so it isn't the greatest come-on line of all time, but I'm lonely too, right? I notice something different about Crash. Normally when the customers at the Big Top talk to you they tend to look at your you-know-whats, but he looks me straight in the eye as if just because I'm a topless waitress doesn't mean I'm not an interesting person in my own right. We get talking. A whole ships-that-pass-in-the-night thing happens.

And three weeks later we're getting hitched in Las Vegas. Who said romance was dead?

Crash

Something had changed while I was inside. Standards had fallen. Eight years before, a guy knew where he stood in life and in business. It was rough now and then, it was tough most all the time, but at least you knew where you stood.

Do this, and you're OK. Do that, and you're not. Do that twice, and they may just find you floating face down in the local reservoir. It was an old-fashioned way of doing things, but it worked.

Now it was different. My ex-business partner, a fink called Gatz, had disappeared. I could have gone after him and disappeared him for good, but that seemed kind of pointless. Besides, I never would have found the slippery little creep.

One night with Ottoleen, the new Mrs Lopez, we got to talking about Sam. I told her that it was bugging me that I had no idea where my boy was. She asked me if I wanted to look after him myself and I had to admit that the idea didn't grab me – I don't have the kind of lifestyle that would suit a young kid. Come to think of it, I didn't even know how old he was these days.

No, I just wanted to know that he was OK and someone was looking out for him, to put my mind at rest. We talked it through. The next day, we headed west.

Back in my old hangouts, I asked around. The word was that Sam had gone to Europe with some English sister of Galaxy's who had turned up at the funeral. There was another rumour – something about a will, something about my old lady having been a lot richer when she was dead than she had been when she was alive.

We got to thinking, Ottoleen and me. Life was kind of empty. The idea of my own flesh and blood growing up to be a little snot-nosed Englishman singing 'God Save the Queen' and wearing a bowler hat suddenly made my skin crawl. I began to get these feelings, these yearnings.

The cash? OK, I admit it – if there was some cash coming loose, I'd have me some of that too.

8

Matthew

The next day we discovered how seriously Sam was taking the whole girl thing.

We met up in the park as usual. He slipped into the lavatory for his daily sex change. But when he came out, he looked a mess – even by the low standards of Sam Lopez.

Something seemed to have happened inside his shirt. First I thought he had decided to smuggle a couple of footballs into school. Then he took off his jacket and undid his shirt.

The three of us stared at him, dumbstruck.

'Will someone give us a hand with these hooks?' He said, twisting a hand behind his back.

'Sam.' It was Jake who spoke first. 'You're wearing a bra.'

'Yup. An enhanced bra, if you must know. El gave it to me. She was worried that I might be hassled by other girls on account of my flat chest.'

'You don't think that's going a bit far?' Tyrone asked. 'What, turn down the offer of free gazungas? Are you crazy?'

I glanced at my watch. We were late again. 'What do I have to do to fasten it?' I said.

Sam turned his back. There was this fiddly little clasp thing which I tried to hook up.

'Hang on,' said Jake. 'You're all out of whack at the front.' He tried to correct Sam's chest, as Tyrone stood by, laughing.

'Get off my tits!' Sam shouted.

It was then that we realised that we were not alone.

Miss Wheeler-Carrington

Well! I hardly have words to express what I saw that morning.

The same three boys that I had seen the previous morning bullying that poor little blonde girl, were at it again. Only this time they were – well, suffice it to say that their hands were in places that they should not be.

'Would you mind telling me exactly what you are doing?' I said in my most forbidding voice. The three boys jumped back, looking guilty and embarrassed.

'It's not what it seems,' the fat one said.

The blonde girl was buttoning herself up after her ordeal. 'They're sex maniacs, these boys,' she said. 'I tell you, ma'am, they just can't keep their hands off me.'

I was slightly surprised at the light-hearted tone of her voice, but I decided that, as a responsible citizen, I had no alternative but to report this incident to the authorities.

Things have come to a pretty pass if one innocent girl can't make her way to school without being...molested.

PC Chivers

As it happens, I do recollect a lady entering the station with a small dog – plump, waddling, with mad, bulging eyes. And the dog didn't look much better!

No, sorry, my little joke. There was certainly a complaint at about that time concerning a group of boys 'messing around', as the lady put it, with a girl in the park. As the newest officer at the station, I was asked to investigate.

Steve Forrester

She was a force for good, that Sam Lopez. Mrs Cartwright had warned me that she had had a chequered educational career in the States and had hinted that the family background had been unstable. Well, all I can say is, there must have been something in the London air that changed her character.

I'll admit she was a bit feisty, albeit a little lippy sometimes. But she was always eager to contribute to the class discussions. Although she wasn't a particularly brilliant student – her view that punctuation 'sucked', grammar was 'for the birds' and spelling 'bummed her out big time' suggested a motivational problem in English – she had energy and confidence which soon communicated itself to the other girls in the class.

A particular problem with this age group is that a small number of boys who are generally uncooperative and unhelpful in class can drag the keener girl students down to their level. Sam dealt with this brilliantly. If one of the boys was chatting or sniggering while she was answering a question, she would give him that special Lopez look – a full, direct burn-out of a stare – and the words or laughter would fizzle out. This, after all, was the girl who had put Gary Laird in his place.

With anyone else it might have been called threatening, but with this little American girl it was something different. Confidence, self-assertion. A positive attitude.

No, I'm happy to say that Sam Lopez was already on her way to being one of the star pupils of Year Eight.

Charley

When Elena breezed into class with this el massivo sports watch, we thought she was having a laugh.

But here's a thing about El. She doesn't do laughs, particularly when there's a danger of the laugh being on her.

'Everyone's wearing them in the States,' she said. 'Big watches are the next big thing. Isn't that right, Sam?' Sitting next to her, Sam raised her left arm and pointed slowly and dramatically to her own sports watch. 'Need I say more?' she said.

'But they're boys' watches,' said Katie Farrell, another Year Eight girl who had been earwigging the conversation.

'Not Stateside they ain't,' said Sam. 'All the Hollywood babes are wearing them these days.'

'Where did you get it, Elena?' Katie asked.

El shrugged, suddenly the fashion icon of Year Eight. 'Sports shop,' she said.

I glanced at Zia. There have been some weird crazes at Bradbury Hill, but big, clunky sports watches?

That was the Sam effect. Suddenly all the girls wanted to be like her.

And there was no doubt about it – she liked the attention. That day she started telling us all sorts of things about the way things were in America.

Basically her message was that girls are the new guys. They were learning that the best way of dealing with boys was to be like them – talk to them in the only language they understand.

'Check this.' Sam was talking to a group of us in the playground that morning. 'The way you girls stand is way too apologetic, too' – she gave a sort of joke sneer – 'female.'

'What's wrong with female?' Elena asked.

Sam gave her the look.

'Sorree,' she said.

'See what I mean?' Sam smiled. 'Give someone the old eyeball and suddenly you're in charge. You should try it sometime.'

'If we go round staring at boys, they'll just think we fancy them,' said Elena.

A couple of Year Nine boys were wandering past, chatting. When one of them glanced at Sam, she gave him the look. He seemed to wince as if he had been hit by a paper pellet, then hurried on. 'See?' said Sam. 'Do it right and they get the message. Now, standing.'

She stood, legs slightly apart, arms hanging loosely

at her side. Then she twitched her shoulders and sort of grabbed herself at the front of her skirt as if she were adjusting herself down there.

We laughed.

'No way can we do that,' I said. 'It's beyond vulgar.'

'Vulgar is good,' said Sam. 'Vulgar is the new polite. Now, how many of you can belch?'

Jake

Suddenly all the girls in Year Eight were coming on like Robert de Niro. It was weird. Two days at Bradbury Hill and already Sam was a damned role model and the girls, even shy ones like Zia Khan, were swaggering about, hitching their crotches and staring threateningly at any boy who dared to look at them.

Matthew

Something was going badly wrong with Operation Samantha. The idea had been that Sam would find out some really useful secrets from the girls – stuff that we could use against them.

Instead, he had gone over to the other side. He hardly bothered to talk to us now. There was no doubt about it – he was having a ball as a girl.

At first I thought it was just the crazy novelty of the situation that had put a spring in his step, a new and unfamiliar smile on his face. Then it occurred to me that dressing up in a skirt and pretending to be someone that he wasn't had done something else for Sam.

Suddenly, he was no longer this tragic kid whose mother had died and whose life had been turned upside down. Girl Sam was happier, more straightforward and open than Boy Sam, and had virtually none of his problems.

Then again, maybe the reason why he was having such a good time was simpler. He was getting away with it. Time and again he would say or do something in class which, if he had been a boy, would have landed him in big trouble. But, now he was a girl, it was all fine. 'Excellent, Sam,' Steve would go. 'Good work.'

As Sam himself would say, 'Go figure.'

Jake

You know what I think? It was his new breasts that did it. They were the final straw. As soon as Sam put on that fake bra and filled out my sister's shirt just like he was a real girl, he was gone. He just grew into himself with those breasts.

Elena

The watch thing was wild. I'm one of those people who likes to set trends. Now every girl in my year had only one thought – where can I get myself one of those hot sports watches that Elena Griffiths has got? Of course, Sam had one too but, much as I loved her, she wasn't a Bradbury Hill fashion icon like me.

Another great thing about that second day. Sam looked terrific in the padded bra I gave her. She seemed to blossom – like her face was no longer closed up and she was laughing and joking as if she had been at the school for years.

I was pleased about that. I like to give. The way I saw it, Sam was part of our gang, but I was her real best friend. Sharing a bra creates a special bond.

Mrs Cartwright

Most mornings I make what I call a tour during breaktime – to show my face, as it were.

On this occasion, I was rather taken aback to see that the girls of Year Eight were assembled in the centre of the play area, engaged in what appeared to be some sort of game. They stood in two lines, crouched forward in a distinctly unladylike pose. As I approached, I heard a high-pitched American voice scream a series of numbers. The group then ran in different directions. Charley Johnson emerged at the front carrying what appeared to be a ball. She threw it hard at someone at the back of the group whom I now saw was the American girl, Sam Lopez.

Sam gave a whoop as she caught the ball, jinked her way through the girls, sprinted to the science-block end of the play area and then screamed like a banshee, 'Touchdooooooown!'

The spectators – most of the school, that is – seemed to find this inordinately amusing and began to applaud.

One of the older boys – Mark Kramer, I think – shouted, 'Way to go, Sam baby!'

I had seen and heard quite enough. Walking briskly towards where the Year Eight girls were gathered, making a fuss of the American girl, I asked them, in none too gentle a tone, what exactly they thought they were doing.

It was Sam Lopez who stepped forward to answer. 'Football, ma'am,' she said. 'Real football. American football.'

Frankly, I was less than impressed by the tone in which she addressed me. She stood, what I call limbering slightly, arms hanging by her sides, looking me straight in the eye.

I said firmly, 'You all know that there is a strict regulation that no ball games are allowed in the play area.'

Elena Griffiths picked up the ball and handed it to Sam.

'Ain't no ball, ma'am,' said Sam, with an unmistakable smirk on her face. 'It's a jacket taped up in a plastic bag.'

Briefly, I was lost for words and, in that moment of hesitation, something odd and rather distasteful happened.

Sam Lopez gave a sort of twitch of the shoulders, then seemed to ...well, adjust herself in the crotch area. She looked around her and, as if at a signal, the other girls performed similar gestures, so that soon the whole of

Year Eight's girl contingent was twitching and scratching at themselves like monkeys, all the while staring at me in a way that I found quite what I call disconcerting.

'Jackets are not for playing football, Sam,' I said eventually. 'If you wish to play sport – and I'm all in favour of girls taking exercise – I would ask you to book the sports field in the normal manner.'

Sam tugged at herself again. 'Yes, ma'am,' she said. Point made, I turned back to the main entrance, looking neither left nor right at the crowd that had gathered. The impromptu game of football broke up, but I had the odd sense that my authority had been undermined.

I was going to have to keep an eye on that little Sam Lopez.

Mark

It was the coolest thing you ever saw – this crazy blonde girl in Year Eight could run and throw like a guy. She had all her friends playing American football. Then, when old Carthorse came grinning with fury into the play area, they stood up to her like some kind of wild bunch, totally hard, totally cool. It takes a lot to impress Mark Kramer, but I was impressed.

At the end of break, I wandered over to Elena Griffiths, the weirdo who had once stalked me when I was out with Tasha.

'Hi, Ellie,' I said.

She blushed sweetly. 'My friends call me El,' she said, going into full eyelid-batting mode.

'Whatever,' I said. 'I have a little personal request.'

She smiled, as if she knew what I was going to ask.

'Mention me to Sam, will you?' I tried not to sound too keen and full-on. 'I'd like to talk to her sometime.'

'Sam, why Sam?' Elena sounded annoyed.

'She's your best friend, isn't she?'

Elena gave a little snort. 'Yeah, and that's why I want to keep her away from people who behave like dorks!'

She stormed off.

What was that all about?

Mrs Burton

I got the call that morning at the office. Mr Durkowitz sounded worryingly apologetic. There had been a breach of security, a snafu, he said.

'What precisely was a snafu when it was at home?' I asked.

Durkowitz said it stood for Situation Normal: All – and then used a swear word which I never thought I would hear from the lips of a lawyer.

'Go on,' I said coldly.

'Tony Lopez, the father of Sam, has been in touch with the office. It seems he's a free man.'

'Ah.'

'Someone in the office appears to have told him that the kid was living in London with his aunt.'

'That was the snafu.'

'Not exactly. The person also confirmed that Sam was in line for a big inheritance.'

'What exactly are you telling me?' I asked.

Durkowitz made a clicking noise with his teeth. 'My guess is that our friend Crash Lopez will soon be on his way to London.'

I was letting the bad news sink in when Durkowitz filled the silence.

'He's not violent or anything,' he said. 'He's just a small-time hood.'

'Oh, that's fine then,' I said, hoping he would pick up the sarcasm in my voice.

'But, maybe just to be on the safe side, you might have a word with the police in London,' said Durkowitz. 'Tell them to keep a lookout for a small, swarthy guy with an American accent and a bad attitude.'

Coldly, I thanked him for his help.

'You're welcome, Mrs Burton,' he said, and hung up.

Jeb Durkowitz

Hey, I was only trying to help. I wasn't too crazy about the idea of Lopez flying off to Europe, but there's a limit to what a lawyer can do. There was no need for Mrs Burton to give me that old British cold shoulder.

The way I saw it, I had done my duty. I closed the file. Of course, if there was some kind of custody battle upcoming, my firm would be ready and willing to represent their interests.

Mr Burton

I was ironing when Mary called from the office. She is not easily moved to panic, so when she told me to double-lock the front door, I knew that we had a serious problem.

Crash Lopez would soon be on his way to London, she said. We needed to decide what to say to him and, equally important, what to tell Sam.

It was time for a family conference and Mary said she would come home early that evening.

Elena

A lot of people would have been upset if the boy they thought happened to like them quite a lot came up and said he wanted to hook up with their best friend, who was a lot less good-looking than them and totally flat-chested into the bargain.

Luckily, I'm not like that. I'll admit that when Marky Mark asked me about Sam and tried to get me to set him up with her, I was a bit, shall we say, peed off at first. Then I realised that, ever since the Cameron Diaz thing, I had been thinking about him less.

Obviously, he had just used me to pull Tasha. If he could be that mean – that sad – there was no future in any relationship between us anyway. I was so over Mark. End of story.

So I took Sam aside and mentioned, casual as you like, that Mark Kramer fancied her.

Her reaction surprised me. She was actually rather angry. She said she didn't know who this guy was and didn't care anyway. He could just butt out and mind his own business.

When I asked her if she had a boyfriend back in the States, she got even angrier, storming about the place, saying that she didn't have boyfriends, and never would have, that having boyfriends was totally gay and ridiculous.

Er, gay? I'm like, huh?

It was only later, when first Charley and then Zia told her that every girl at Bradbury Hill wanted to go out with Mark Kramer, that she began to lighten up. When some of the girls asked her if it was true about her and Mark, she shrugged in a way that any sane person would take as a yes. I think she quite liked the idea that a boy who was good-looking (admittedly in a vacant, stupid, floppy-haired sort of way) was interested in her.

The three of us went round to Charley's place that night. I told them that I had set up the Sam and Mark thing, that it was all down to me. They were impressed by how well I had dealt with the situation and I have to admit that, looking back on it, I handled it all pretty well.

Call me Cupid.

9

Matthew

Sam was having such a good time as a girl that he was almost out of control.

As the four of us made our way home that evening, he was running on at the mouth about how great Zia, Charley and Elena were, how talking to them was just so different from talking to guys.

'Like, feelings,' he suddenly said. 'It's OK to talk about what's really going on inside. I really dig that.'

'We do that too.' Jake was walking ahead, hands in pockets. 'I talk to Ty about feelings all the time, don't I, Ty?'

'Yeah,' Tyrone muttered unconvincingly. 'We really share.'

'And old Zed – she is just totally ace,' Sam went on. 'I told her about some of the sixties rock bands I like and, you know what? She's heard of Jim Morrison. She's into Hendrix. She's got a Doors playlist. How cool is that?'

'Doors?' said Jake. 'What exactly are the Doors?'

'Only the best band in the history of time,' said Sam. 'Another thing. We've agreed that we're all going to keep diaries this term,' Sam went on happily. 'Everything that happens, all our secrets – it's all going to be in there.'

'Diaries?' A look of real disgust crossed Tyrone's face. 'That is such a girl thing, Sam.'

'What kind of secrets?' I asked.

Sam gave what can only be described as a giggle as we entered the park. 'Oh, only, for instance, that a certain Mark Kramer wants to meet me.'

'Kramer? The Lower-Sixth guy?' Jake asked.

'Yup,' said Sam. 'And the word is that he is hot-hot-hot for a certain Sam Lopez. The other girls are sooo jealous. Everybody wants to be Mark's girl but he has only eyes for me. Talk about romantic.'

'Sam,' I said, as gently as I could. 'Sam, he's a boy.'

'Correction,' said Sam chirpily. 'He's a hunk – the hunk of the Lower Sixth. Mark and Sam. Sam and Mark. It even sounds right.'

'But what do you want to go out with a boy for?' Tyrone asked.

Sam shrugged. 'Fun. Laughs. Sharing things. And, after that who knows?'

We were so shocked by what we were hearing that none of us noticed the policeman walking towards us.

PC Chivers

The three boys and a girl, fitting the description I had been given, were in earnest conversation with one another in the vicinity of the playground shelter. I walked up to them and, to my surprise, they kept on talking.

'Afternoon, kids,' I said. 'Is everything all right here?'
The girl answered. She said everything was very all right.

I mentioned that I had received a complaint of inappropriate behaviour from a group of four kids of about their age.

'Inappropriate behaviour?' said the tall, skinny boy with the big nose. 'What sort of inappropriate behaviour?'

'Messing around,' I said. 'Upsetting ladies walking their dogs.'

'OK, officer. We'll look out for those kids,' said the girl, who seemed to be American.

'All right then,' I said. 'On your way.'

All in all, I think I handled the situation in a satisfactory manner.

Tyrone

It was not exactly a normal end to the school day. First of all, Sam coming on all romantic about Mark Kramer, then the very same young police guy who had warned us after the Great Burger Bill Disaster turning up in the park. I got the weird sense that somehow things were just about to go seriously wrong.

At the park gates, we decided to split up. Jake and me would go home and Matt and Sam would take a couple of turns around the block before doubling back to the park for Sam to change back into a boy. With a bit of luck, PC Stickybeak would have moved on.

Matthew

Sam was flipping. Two days of being a girl, being given a new pair of falsies and winning the heart of Mark Kramer had done nothing for his sanity, and the tangle with the law had wound him up still further.

'Let's go check out the park!' He danced ahead of me, punching the palm of his hand with his fist. 'Let's make a little mayhem here – let's go kick some ass.'

I told him that personally I didn't need any more trouble on account of the fact that whenever a little mayhem was made, it was me that got the blame.

'Whoa, there.' Sam laughed crazily. 'Is my little cousin losing his nerve here? Maybe Operation Samantha turned out to be a little hot for him.'

'You might be right,' I said. 'It's getting sort of messy, isn't it – all this girlie stuff? I've been thinking that perhaps we should just fess up and get on with our lives. What can they do? Kill us?'

Sam had stopped dancing. 'Easy, Matthew,' he said. 'You asked me to do a week at Bradbury Hill. We've still got three days to go.'

We turned the corner towards the park. I was just about to tell Sam that the joke was meant to be on the girls but that somehow nothing had changed, when I saw something that made me stop in my tracks.

My mother was driving towards us. She had been looking for a parking space and had found one fifty metres from where we stood. As she stepped out of the car, she saw us.

'Don't say a word,' I murmured. 'Just do what I say.'

'What?' said Sam, then noticed my mother. 'Uh-oh.'

'Turn round slowly and naturally,' I said. To my surprise, he did so without a murmur of complaint. 'Here we go again,' I said, then slung my right arm casually around his shoulders. Briefly, he tried to wrestle his way free, but I held him firmly and he relaxed.

'You are going to pay for this big time,' he muttered.

'Just stay like this until we turn the corner,' I said.

We were almost there when I glanced behind me.

Mum was standing beside her car, staring after us.

We turned the corner. I released my grip and Sam jumped away from me.

'You are sick, Matthew Burton,' he said. 'How come you're always hitting on me these days?'

I smiled wearily. 'Now who's losing his nerve?' I said.

Mrs Burton

As if the day hadn't provided enough shocks, it seemed that Matthew had discovered girls. As I watched him scurry away, a little ponytailed blonde under his arm, I experienced the sort of feeling that every mother knows when her child makes its first step into adulthood – a little sad, of course, but relieved too.

Matthew with a girlfriend. I laughed quietly.

When I reached 23 Somerton Gardens, David was in the kitchen – no surprise there. He has this theory that, at times of crisis, it is important for family unity that we all have a good meal together. Tonight it was going to be paella. As I entered, he scooped some red sauce stuff onto a spoon and held it up to me.

'Has this got enough flavour, do you think?' he asked, his face a picture of anxiety.

'Matthew has a girlfriend,' I said. 'I've just seen them. I don't think they noticed me. Some little long-haired blonde.'

David stood there, still holding out the spoon.

'Matthew? It's not possible. I mean, isn't he a bit young?' I told him kids started early these days. Maybe it was a good thing, I said. It would give him confidence.

'Who was she?' he asked.

'Probably someone from his class.' I tasted the sauce and told him it needed more salt. 'Have you ever...talked to him?' I asked.

David stirred something in a saucepan, looking worried. 'You mean talk as in...talk? The talk?' He shook his head. 'Not exactly.'

I told him it was time for the talk. He nodded miserably. It was only when we heard the boys at the front door that I realised we had completely forgotten to discuss the imminent arrival of Sam's father.

Matthew

I had assumed that there had to be some kind of crisis for Mum to leave her office so early and, when I saw both of them standing looking worried in the kitchen, I thought we were in for some heavy news.

But it turned out that something else was on their minds.

'Oh, was that you I saw near the park? Mum had a weird half-smile on her face that I have learned is a sign that she's trying to be playful.

'Park?' I said. 'I don't think so.'

'I could have sworn I saw you with a girl.'

I shrugged guiltily. 'Nah,' I muttered. 'Must have been someone else.'

'So you were with Sam?' my father asked.

I glanced across at Sam and in that instant, I knew what was coming. Ever since I had put my arm around him, he had been waiting for his revenge.

'Nope. I was with Jake and Tyrone,' he said. 'I wanted to give ole Matt a little,' – he winked at me – 'quality time, know what I mean?'

'There's no need to be embarrassed,' said my father. 'It's quite natural. Who is she?'

'Yeah,' said Sam. 'Who's the babe?'

I panicked. 'Sss…Sss…Simone,' I said. 'She's in my class.'

My mother smiled. 'I never heard you mention a Simone in your class.'

'I hadn't really noticed her before,' I murmured. 'I don't want to talk about her.'

'We do,' said Sam, really enjoying himself now. 'Tell us what she's like, Matthew.'

My parents were both looking at me expectantly.

'Well, she's quiet and reasonably bright and maybe a bit shy.'

'And a great looker, ain't that a fact?'

I narrowed my eyes. If it was the last thing I ever did, I was going to get Sam back for this. 'Yes,' I said

116

coldly. 'She's quite pretty – in a very girly, feminine sort of way.'

At this point, Mum nudged my father. 'Well, I've got a couple of calls to make from upstairs,' she said, giving him this meaningful glance, and walked quickly out of the kitchen.

Mr Burton

I have always regarded myself as something of a communicator but, between you and me, that birds-and-bees chat with Matthew and Sam was not a great success. Certain words and phrases, of an intimate nature, came out sounding peculiar – as if somehow they had never been used before.

Matthew kept on trying to interrupt me, telling me that he knew it all, that there wasn't any need to go into any of this, but unfortunately Sam seemed very innocent in these matters and asked questions that frankly I found increasingly difficult to answer.

Matthew

No no no no no NO! Not that! Not in the kitchen! Not from my father! Please stop!

As Dad tried in his desperate, fumbling way to tell us all about sex, he looked increasingly miserable. There were long, awkward silences. Whenever he had to use words that he found embarrassing – 'condom', 'erection', 'sperm', 'vagina' – he sort of winced as if just saying the words was causing him physical pain.

Sam, I don't have to tell you, was having the time of his life. On and on he went, asking questions that made me want to hide under the kitchen table.

'You mean the guy gets his...And the girl...Explain that to me again, Mr Burton.' On and on he went. 'So what exactly *is* safe sex?'

That was it, I decided. That...was...it. War had been declared – officially.

After the Great Sex Talk, we went upstairs, Sam frowning to himself as if still turning over in his brain the fascinating but troubling new things he had just discovered about boys and girls and their bodies. We went into my room, closed the door, and he fell on my bed, face in the pillow, hammering the mattress with delight.

'Sam!' I grabbed the back of his shirt and yanked him up. When he looked at me there were tears of laughter in his eyes.

I couldn't help it. I wanted to be angry, but soon I was laughing too.

Poor Dad. If only he knew.

10

Crash

It was one helluva flight. Ottoleen had never been on an aeroplane before and, in one of those crazy magazines that she gets every week, she had read that flying at altitude can have a serious effect if you happen to have silicone implants in your body.

Ottoleen has silicone implants in her body. Up top, if you know what I mean. In fact, she probably has more silicone in her body than body.

For nine hours, she sat beside me, arms across herself. 'They're gonna burst, Crash,' she whispered. 'That's what happens, you know. Bang! All over everybody. I just know they're going to pop.'

I gave her a drink. Then another. By the time we started our descent into London, we were, shall we say, feeling no pain.

Ottoleen

'Jeez, Crash,' I'm saying over and over. 'This had better be worth it.'

To take my mind off the flight, I try to think of what we were going to do with the reward, inheritance, whatever.

We'll have this big, classy ranch-style mansion with huge bathrooms and gold taps, just near Hollywood, so I can pursue my acting career. We'll have land and horses and loads of maids and stuff, and they'll treat me real respectful, like, 'Morning, Mrs Lopez' and, 'Will that be all, Mrs Lopez?'

I guess the brat Sam will have to be around seeing as he was the reason we hit pay-dirt in the first place, but I imagine him as a kind of sassy, bright, zany kid who says all those wacky teenage things without ever being a total pain in the you-know-what – kind of like Macaulay Culkin before he went all weird and got married and stuff.

It's going to be worth it, I say to myself, holding on tight – to my chest (these things cost money!). It's all going to be totally worth it.

Zia

I was a bit disappointed to hear that Sam was falling for Mark Kramer. It was just so corny – I mean, everyone fell for Mark Kramer.

Sam, I had thought, had more taste. For instance, when we had talked, it hadn't been about the usual stuff but about music. She wrote down the names of guitarists that I should check out – not just Hendrix, Clapton, Plant, the people I had read about, but others like Albert Lee, Jeff Beck, Scotty Moore, James Burton. She wrote out a list of sixties bands I should listen to and promised to share her music collections with me.

It was weird. She seemed so totally modern, yet, if I talked about trance, techno or drum 'n' bass, she shook her head as if she just didn't want to know about any of that.

Musically, she was about a zillion years old, yet totally up to date. I didn't mind – in fact, when I got home, I got out my phone and listened to the Doors again.

Somehow none of this squared with her going all goo-goo over Mark Kramer. How could someone so cool, so different, be such a cliché when it came to love?

Tyrone

That was the night when life at home became even more complicated.

My mum had become obsessed with the idea that she had to do something about me before it was too late. As far as she was concerned, I was a walking collection of everything that's ever been wrong with a teenager. I was overweight, I was underperforming at school. And she wasn't too keen on the friends I hung out with either.

She had come up with this idea that I needed private tuition a couple of evenings a week. After supper, she rang Matthew's mum, assuming that she would have the names of some tutors – parents of 'problem children' should stick together, right? Instead she got an ear-load of stuff about Matthew's new girlfriend.

There's something about the parents in my area that seems to make them dead competitive. They have to compare their precious kids all the time – when they first walk, when they talk, how they are doing at school, what really interesting hobbies they have, the cute things they have said, how they are doing at sports or music, how many friends they have, the exams they have passed. On and on and on it goes.

This is a game that my mother feels she has to play and, tragically, it's one she always loses. Sometimes I hear her talking to another parent on the telephone. 'He gets on with everybody, does Ty,' she'll say desperately, or, 'What he doesn't know about the Internet just isn't worth knowing.' In the world of parents, this kind of thing spells out one message, loud and clear: I'M DOING MY BEST, BUT THE FACT IS MY SON IS A COMPLETE AND UTTER LOSER.

That night, talking to Mrs Burton, she was introduced to yet another area where she could feel bad about her son.

Girls. Matthew Burton had a girlfriend. I listened from the first floor, not believing what I was hearing.

'Quite smitten?' Mum laughed in a fake-jolly, ha-ha-ha-ha, dying-inside way. 'Funnily enough,' she dropped her voice. 'Tyrone has been showing an interest in the daughter of friends of mine, the Laverys. He's a successful barrister, you know.'

I sunk my head in my hands, then wearily made my way back to my room to await the visit that would surely come.

Mrs Sherman

Tyrone is slightly young for his age. That's why he has difficulty losing weight. It's puppy fat. I'm sure it will just fall away when he reaches sixteen.

I decided to have a chat with him – or rather a chat with the back of his head while he played a game on his laptop.

'I hear that Matthew has a girlfriend,' I said casually.

'First I've heard of it,' said Tyrone.

'She's very pretty, apparently. And bright too. Simone. D'you know her?'

I noticed that Tyrone had stopped playing the game.

'Nope,' he said.

'I'm just worried about your falling behind, Tyrone. You'd be so much happier if you were spending time with a girl.' Tyrone played on, ignoring me. 'Perhaps I should arrange that tea with the Laverys,' I said. 'Juliana's always asking about you.'

Tyrone made one of his usual, unhelpful grunting noises.

'Girls are fun,' I said encouragingly. 'You could, you know, go to the cinema together. I'm sure Juliana has a lot more to offer than those boys you spend all your time with.'

Tyrone switched off his game, sighed heavily and turned in his seat. 'Mum, I don't want a girlfriend,' he said. 'I've got nothing to talk about with girls. I'm not interested.'

'Be interested.' I spoke more firmly. 'I'd be a lot happier if there were at least some sign of early dating in your life. I don't know what I'd do if you turned into one of those men who sit all alone in their bedsits in front of a laptop and eat TV dinners and don't wash as often as they could. That would make me very, very sad as your mother, Tyrone.'

He groaned, long and low.

'Will you just try?' I said. 'Meet Juliana. She might be the one. And if she's not, you can keep an eye out for another one. Will you? For me?'

He nodded.

I smiled and kissed him on the top of his head. He's all right, Tyrone. He just needs a little motherly help to bring him out of his shell.

Tyrone

Simone? It could only be Sam. Now what had he done?

Mrs Cartwright

I had a quiet word with Steve Forrester in the staffroom. It was just what I call a pre-emptive warning.

'The Year Eight girls,' I said. 'How are they doing?'

He replied that it was early days but that he was pleased by the way his class was behaving. The girls he said were 'lively and interested'.

When I mentioned the ball game in the play area, he actually smiled.

'There's a difference between lively and loutish,' I said, retaining my good humour with some difficulty. 'Miss Fisher reported that while she was rebuking young Katie Spicer, another of the girls actually broke wind – quite noisily too.'

Steve said he would make sure that Year Eight understood the importance of discipline.

'The American girl, Sam Lopez,' I said. 'She's rather what I call full of herself, isn't she?'

Steve said that Sam was fine – a little feisty, but basically a good kid.

And I believed him. Twenty years' experience as a teacher and I actually believed him.

Matthew

By now Operation Samantha had gone belly up. The Shed Gang was history, the Bitches forgotten. Everything had changed.

But nothing changed more than Sam Lopez. In class he was at the front, his little ink-stained hand in the air with the other swots and pencil-pushers. Some of the teachers – Ward in maths, Fisher in art – became impatient with him on the grounds that he often put up his hand when he had no idea what the answer was. He just wanted to talk.

But Steve Forrester was still his number one fan. 'There's nothing wrong with a bit of enthusiasm,' he would say if one of us laughed at some lame answer he gave. 'At least Sam is trying, unlike some people I could mention.' And then, when the teacher wasn't looking, Sam would turn in his seat and stick out his tongue.

Yes, you heard that right. He stuck out his tongue. He may have been teaching the girls how to walk and talk and look and chew like a boy, but he was moving even faster in the opposite direction. A few days in a skirt and Sam was essentially a girl in his gestures: the way he talked all the time, and bumped up against his friends when they were walking down the corridor, or touched their arm when telling them some little titbit of gossip.

A weird and frightening fact began to emerge – something so strange and uncomfortable that none of us actually mentioned it, although each of us knew it was true. Sam was changing. He was actually becoming nicer, easier to talk to, human.

Jake

I still thought he could turn at any moment. /remembered what happened at Burger Bill's after I made a joke about his dad, even if no one else did.

He didn't do much to improve the girls either. They just talked even more than they once did. Oh, and they were all wearing these ridiculous sports watches – in fact, the craze had reached right up to the Sixth-Form girls.

If you need any evidence about how pathetic girls can be, there it is. Sports watches. This years fashion accessory. Do me a favour.

Zia

This was the big moment. Even now, when I think about it, I get goosebumps down my spine.

During breaktime, I mentioned to Sam that I had been listening to the Doors. She laughed and asked me what my favourite track was.

'"People Are Strange",' I said.

'You're kidding,' she said. 'Not "Light My Fire"? Everyone usually goes for that.'

'Well, I like "People Are Strange". I've worked out the chords. I can play it on the guitar.'

She looked at me as if she had just heard the best news ever. Then, to my utter amazement, she began to sing.

It's a weird song, about being unwanted, about how people look different and ugly when you're alone in the world, and Sam's voice – high, with a hint of rasp in it – went with the lyrics and the melody.

I couldn't help it. The music gathered me up and carried me along. I found myself singing out the guitar line, cutting across the vocal melody with the staccato rhythm, the minor chords changing to major at the chorus, hitting it with a high, spooky harmony, strange and haunting like the song itself.

As we finished the chorus, there was silence for a few seconds. That had been a good noise we had just made between us – an excellent noise, in fact.

Sam gave a little laugh, almost embarrassed at how great it had sounded. Then she started the next verse. More confident now, I joined in.

We smiled as we sang. Something truly astonishing was happening. Nearby, people glanced in our direction – I mean, nobody sings two-part harmonies in the play area of Bradbury Hill – but then, just as they were about to laugh at us or tell us to shut up, the music gathered them up too.

By the time we reprised the first verse, a small crowd had gathered around us. When we finished, there was a smattering of applause.

'When did you practise that?' someone asked.

'We didn't,' I said.

'Musical instinct,' said Sam, shaking her head.

We moved away from one another, almost as if we each needed time to work out what had just happened.

I couldn't stop thinking about it, hearing the music in my head for the rest of the day.

Crash

It was grey at the airport. Outside it was raining in that typically British way, thin and indecisive. There were too many people. When Ottoleen and me asked anyone a simple question, they looked at us like we'd just crawled out from under a stone.

'Here's the thing,' I said as we waited in line for the taxi. 'We rent a car. We track the kid down. We grab him. We get the hell outta this dump and beat it back to civilisation.'

'Gotta sleep.' Ottoleen was swaying gently. She was never great at holding her liquor, that one. 'Take me to a hotel, Crash.'

Normally when I hear these words from the gorgeous mouth of a young babe, I don't need to give the matter too much thought, but right now I had family business to attend to.

'We check in, then we rent a car. Then—'

But Ottoleen had rested her head on my shoulder and was making those little mewing noises that she knows I can't resist. 'Kitty's sleepee,' she said.

'All right,' I snapped. 'I'll get you to a hotel.'

'Miew-miew' went Ottoleen's lovely lips as, eyes closed, she nodded her head in thanks.

I noticed that the family in front of us, Mom and Pop and a couple of pug-ugly, red-haired juniors, all of them glowing red from their holiday, were staring at us.

'You got some kinda problem?' I asked them, giving them my best you-don't-mess-with-this-guy look. They turned an even deeper shade of red and turned away, muttering nervously.

I tell ya, these Brits. No goddam manners.

Mrs Burton

We have always been a no-secrets, let's-sort-this-out-together sort of family, but frankly the whole business of Sam's inheritance, not to mention the fact that his rather odd-sounding father could soon be sniffing about the place, was proving to be something of a problem for David and me.

Term had started so well, with Sam settling into school and Matthew even managing to find himself a girlfriend, that it seemed unwise to upset the boys at this delicate moment. In the end we decided that on this occasion honesty could wait.

I asked David to ring the police, simply to alert them that an undesirable American might be patrolling the area and that they should be aware that there was a possibility of an abduction situation. I'm not sure that they took him quite as seriously as one might have hoped.

PC Chivers

I have a note that a certain Mr Burton rang to express concerns about the activities of a Mr Lopez. I recorded the call in the police log, but told him that the faint possibility of an American gentleman roaming the streets of our constabulary with a view to abducting his son was not one that we could regard as our highest priority, even if he was, as Mr Burton said, 'slightly dodgy'.

I was aware that I had heard the name Burton quite recently. Only later did I make the connection with the incident at Burger Bill's.

Mr Burton

It's very important not to overreact, not to panic on these occasions. I made the call and suggested to Mary that we should all now get on with our lives.

With this in mind, I decided not to mention to her something else that I had noticed. Sam appeared to have plucked his eyebrows.

There was, in fact, something indefinably different about him. Sometimes he touched the arm of the person he was talking to. The way he spoke seemed softer, less abrasive than the old Sam. He used chirpy, un-Sam-like phrases like 'Oh, perlease' or 'I don't think so' or even 'I am so not interested in that'.

At some point every evening, he announced that he had to go upstairs to write his diary.

I confess that I had never thought of Sam Lopez as a diary-keeping sort of person.

Mark

She was just a girl. I kept telling myself that as I saw Sam Lopez over the next couple of days. She's just a kid. Get over it, Mark Kramer.

But I couldn't help myself. I had this empty, sick feeling in the pit of my stomach. Most days, I snuck out of school after lunch for a quick cig, but now I couldn't be bothered. I wanted to see Sam. I wanted to talk to her.

What was going on here? I could have hooked up with any girl at Bradbury Hill, but I had to fall for some little Year Eight Yank who seemed not to give a damn about me.

Maybe that's an exaggeration. I noticed that when I was near her (which was as often as I could arrange), her friends went all giggly and stupid, but I could swear that from the way she glanced in my direction Sam was not exactly unhappy at the attention I was paying her.

But she also made sure she was never alone.

It was a whole day since I had given Elena Griffiths the message for Sam. I knew from the way she was behaving that it had reached her. Mark Kramer is not used to being kept waiting, least of all by a girl. So as Sam and the three girls, including Elena, were fetching their coats at the end of the day, I made as if I just happened to be walking by.

'Hi, Sam,' I said coolly.

She glanced over her shoulder from the coatrack and gave me that long, even look that made my stomach do a triple somersault.

'Yeah?' she said.

'Did you, er, get my message?'

Sam had turned away. 'Might have,' she said as Elena and her two friends nudged one another and giggled. 'So?' I asked.

'We'll see you at the gate, Sam,' Elena said, virtually tugging the other two away with her.

Suddenly it was just us.

'Alone at last.' I gave her the smile. No one can resist the smile.

No one except Sam Lopez.

She took a step nearer to me and, for an instant, I thought she was going to hit me. Instead, she poked me in the chest with her hard little finger.

'Watch it, buddy,' she said in a low, almost threatening voice. 'You're in way over your head.'

She stepped back and stood eyeballing me, hands on hips like some crazy gangster's moll from an old film. 'Back off,' she said. *'Capisce?'*

Then she turned and flounced off down the corridor, her hair swishing behind her like the tail of an angry pony. God, I love that girl. She just gets better and better.

Ottoleen

Crash Lopez is the most masterful guy I've ever been with in my entire life. He is totally, totally focused. I've told him he should write a book one day, *The Crash Lopez Guide to Making Things Happen Even When Everybody in the Whole World Says It's Totally Impossible*. Maybe the title needs a little work, but the message would be loud and clear and just unbelievably inspirational.

Here's the Crash method:

1   Decide what you want to do.
2   Kick some you-know-what.
3   Shout.
4   Kick some more you-know-what.
5   Do it.

So we're in this big, ugly hotel near the airport. We've slept a few hours and just had this kind of headache-nausea-jetlag trying to remind us of our flight.

Crash goes to the desk. 'I need to rent a car,' he says.

The receptionist, one of those Morticia Addams types with dyed black hair and thin, disapproving vowels, looks up from the computer screen she was staring at and says, 'Would that be today, sir?'

I can see Crash losing it already. You don't talk to Crash Lopez like that, you just don't. 'No, I'd like to sit around in this hotel for another week just for the hell of it. Of course today!'

'Yes, sir.' The woman smiles and pushes a telephone that's on the counter a few inches towards him. 'If you would care to ask for the car-rental service, they will be pleased to help you.'

Crash shoots me a look, like do-they-all-talk-like-they've-got-a-poker-up-their-you-know-whats? Then he picks up the receiver and snaps, 'Car rental.'

He talks for, like, five minutes on the phone, giving them all sorts of details. There's a lot of chat about how much the car is going to cost, whether it's a family car, if it has air-conditioning. In the end Crash agrees to take a Nissan on account of the fact that he once had a Nissan back in the States. He asks how long it will take to deliver. They say an hour. He cusses a bit. They seem to be saying that the longer he talks, the later it will be. He hangs up. 'What a country,' he mutters, pushing the phone back to Morticia.

'Thank you, sir,' she says.

An hour later, Crash and me are at the front entrance when this tiny thing, this flea on wheels, pulls up at the kerb. A young, black guy in a tight, shiny suit gets out.

'Mr Lopez,' he says.

Crash looks at the car like the truth is slowly, slowly dawning. 'You're kidding,' he says.

'Your Nissan Micra, sir,' goes the young guy.

'I asked for a Nissan. This ain't no Nissan. This is a toy.' He walks round the car, cursing and calling it names. The driver stands there, looking embarrassed.

So I decide to take action. This is getting us nowhere and it's not as if we have to drive across the country, right? 'It looks snug,' I say. 'I like it.'

'No way is Crash Lopez going to be seen in that tin can.' Crash stands in front of the car and I can see he's weakening.

'No one knows you here,' I say. 'You'll blend in. People will think you're British.'

'And that's a good thing?' says Crash. Then as if he's made up his mind to be reasonable he walks round and gets into the car. For a moment he looks kind of lost. 'Where's the freakin' steering wheel?' he says.

'I think it's on the other side.'

He gets out, walks round, swearing more, then gets into the driver's seat. He wriggles round as if he's been trapped in some kind of foxhole. 'Ah, gimme the keys,' he holds out his hand, staring moodily ahead of him.

The young guy gives him the keys.

Crash turns on the ignition and revs the motor while the porter puts our bags in the back.

'Someone's gonna pay for this,' says Crash as the back door is closed. The porter is sidling up to the open window for his tip when Crash crunches the manual gears and we're out of there, in our crazy little toy car, hopping like a bouncing bean.

See what I mean? That's the Crash Lopez method. He just gets things done.

11

Charley

To tell the truth, the bust-up had been coming for some time. El and Zed are the best of buddies most of the time, but that's because in our little group I stand between them. Just now and then, this huge gulf of difference appears and, for a day or two, we all realise that variety might be the spice of life, but too much variety in a group of three friends can lead to big problems.

Zia is quiet, bright, keeps herself to herself, serious-minded.

Elena is noisy, extrovert. When it comes to school-work, she's the kind of person who, when asked the capital of America, will say, 'Hollywood.'

Back in primary school, we could laugh at how different they were. Now, it seems it matters more and more. The big fallout was waiting to happen – it just needed the smallest spark to set it off, *boom*.

Sam Lopez was that small spark.

Elena had decided that Sam was her project. She has always had these crazes – roller skating, photography, autograph-hunting, basketball – and normally they burn bright for a month or so before fizzling out to be replaced by a new craze.

Ever since Sam had gone back to El's place and been kitted out with a padded bra, El had taken a special interest in her. There was something in the American girl, a sort of weird vulnerability behind her confidence, that seemed to appeal to El. All that could and should have been blown apart when cute-but-clumsy Mark Kramer asked her to set up a date with Sam. Instead, weirdly, it made El feel even closer to Sam – the whole fancying Mark thing was yet another special thing that they could share. Sam was this month's craze.

Unfortunately, on that very same day, something happened. Sam and Zia had this massive musical bonding. At first it was funny the way they skipped about the place warbling like a couple of skylarks or chatting about music and groups no one had ever heard of, but after a while, to be honest, it became kind of irritating. Suddenly, as far as Bradbury Hill's own little singing sisters were concerned, the rest of us had ceased to exist.

Elena took this very, very badly. I noticed her watching them throughout the day, her eyes getting that shifty, narrow look that signals trouble. We had had a plan to go round to Zia's that night, but Elena cancelled, saying she had a headache ('All that singing's done my head in,' was the way she put it).

The next morning, she was in a brighter, harder mood. At breaktime, Zia and Sam were vocalising as usual. Elena, all positive, asked if she could join in. That was when the trouble started.

Elena

All right, so I don't have the best voice. Was that any reason for them to fall about like they had heard the greatest joke ever told (which they hadn't)?

I didn't blame Sam. She's new round here and no one had taken the time to explain to her that Zia Khan may be all innocent and what-you-see-is-what-you-get, but deep down she's a scheming, snooty, mean, devious, uppity, smug, swotty, unfriendly, selfish, moody and generally totally horrible little cow.

So I did it. There, in the playground. I told Zia I'd never really liked her and that I felt sorry for her with her perfect little family and high grades. I thought she was crap at guitar and her voice sounded like a Siamese cat whose tail had been caught in the door. And that was just the warm-up.

Maybe I went a tad too far. Suddenly Zia welled up and ran back to the classroom. As Charley followed her, Sam gave me this puzzled look.

I shrugged coolly. Like, was it something I said?

Jake

Result. There was this big barney in the playground. Tyrone, Matt and me checked it out. Would you believe that it was a full-on cat fight between Elena and Zia and it seemed that Sam was the cause of it all?

When Zia ran off to have a good old cry about it, I caught Sam's eye and gave him a guys-together wink, as if to say, 'That's more like it. We'll have some more of that, please.'

But here's the weird bit. He just blanked me. He had this strange look on his face – it was almost concerned, like he'd got a flood alert going too. Then he just turns and follows Charley Johnson in the direction of the classroom, totally part of the emergency emotional-paramedic squad.

Zia

I walked to the classroom, closed the door behind me and slumped down at one of the desks. I wanted to die. I had thought that Elena and I were friends. It was as if this was what she had been thinking of me all those years, as if everything between us had been nothing but one big lie.

I heard the door open behind me. I sat up, grabbed a book on the desk and pretended to work.

'You OK?' It was Sam.

'I'm—' I was about to tell her that I was just fine but, instead of words, this great, uncontrollable sob just bubbled from inside me. I lost it for a moment. I just couldn't speak.

'Easy.' Sam sat beside me and took my hand. 'Easy.'

She started talking in a quiet, low voice.

'Did I ever tell you about this kid I knew?' she said. 'He was at one of my schools – an OK sort of guy, funny, popular, kind of a friend of mine. But there was this one thing about him. Just now and then, every few weeks or so, he would say something so mean, so ugly, that he'd get into a fight. And here's the weird bit. Because he was small and seemed to go out of his way to annoy people who were bigger and stronger than him, it was usually him that got smeared all over the canvas.'

'Why did he do it?'

It was almost as if when things were going too well that he had to mess them up. He forced people away from him.'

I shrugged. For the life of me, I couldn't see what Sam's story had to do with Elena turning out to be the nastiest, most two-faced so-called friend anyone has ever had.

'So.' Sam sat forward, frowning as if there was something almost painful about the direction her thoughts were leading her. 'I started wondering what caused this guy to act the way he did. I asked around. Turned out that the problem had nothing to do with his friends at all.' She hesitated for a moment.

'What had it got to do with?'

'His dad. My friend's father was kind of out of control, always in trouble with the cops, he was one of those people who go...crashing through life without thinking too much about the effects of what they do. People said that he was a bad father but, the way my friend saw it, he was his dad and that was just the way he was.'

'I still don't understand why he got into fights.'

'One day, when my friend was five, his father did something so bad, so crazy, that his mom kicked him out of the mobile home where they were living. She said he wasn't fit be part of a family, that she never ever wanted to see him again.

'And you know what? She never did, and neither did my friend.'

'That's a really sad story,' I said.

'So the reason why this guy was always causing trouble was simple – he was angry and he was hurt and every day of his life he thought about why his father had left and wondered whether maybe it had been his fault that the family had broken up. For some reason that even he couldn't understand, he got himself punched and punished and tried to hurt other people. Somehow all that pain – real pain, not the stuff that was churning away inside of him – made him feel better for a while.'

I looked at Sam and noticed that there was a strange and distant look in her eyes that I had never seen before.

'You must have known this guy pretty well. Was he your boyfriend or something?'

Sam laughed and seemed to snap out of her mood. 'Nah', she said. 'So here's the bit. My guess is that Elena's got her own problems – maybe not at home but in herself. She's jealous of you – how you get on in class, your friends, maybe even...you and me, the music thing and all. So she wants to hurt you.' She placed a hand on each of my shoulders and looked me in the eyes. 'You've got to slice your own groove in this life.'

I smiled and noticed that, for some weird reason, my heart was beating faster and my mouth was dry. 'Maybe you're right,' I said. 'Poor old El.'

'That's the way to go, babe,' said Sam. 'Slice your own groove.'

It was only later, back at home, that I began to wonder about that word she had used. Babe? *Babe?*

Matthew

Sam was in the strangest mood that day.

'Burger Bill's, guys,' he said when he met us at the school gate. 'I've had way too much raw emotion. I need some action.'

'You're kidding!' Jake laughed. 'We've already had a warning from the police. There's no way that Bill would let us in.'

'Not even if a sweet little girl asked him really nicely?'

'You mean, you want to go to the precinct like that?' I asked. 'In...uniform?'

'Can't risk blowing my cover, can I?' said Sam. 'Who's coming with me?'

I've got to make a confession here. I'd started to miss the old, devilish Sam. I wouldn't have minded having him back the way he was during the holidays. I thought that going along with him on one of his crazy stunts might just remind him how good it was to be a boy, even if he happened to be dressed as a girl.

Jake said he was in, but Tyrone seemed less sure. Normally, he was the least moody of the three of us, but he had been brooding all day. It turned out – Tyrone can never keep a secret for long – that he had been having problems at home and it was all my fault for having this great girlfriend.

As we made our way towards the shopping precinct, I brought Sam up to speed on the situation, but the sympathy he had shown Zia Khan seemed somehow to have disappeared now that he was back among the guys.

'Whoa, so Ty has to get himself a girlfriend now,' he said. 'Boy, that Simone seems to be causing trouble all over.'

Tyrone smiled and led the way to the High Street. His moods never lasted for long.

Crash

We checked into some dive of a hotel on the west of town. Then we started looking. It didn't take us long.

Tyrone

There was a weird atmosphere that evening. Any way we looked at it, we had pulled off a major scam over the past four days. When Sam revealed himself to be a guy at the end of the week there were certain to be some red faces all over Bradbury Hill School.

But, by the way, how exactly was that going to happen? Somehow an easy 'Yah boo, tricked ya!' was unlikely to cover the row that was going to break when Sam abandoned his cute coat-and-skirt uniform, his hairband, his padded bra. At this point it began to dawn on us that we had got our great plan off the ground but that now we had to land it without injury to the crew.

Matthew

Sam walked into Burger Bill's as if he were there every day, pushing the door and plumping himself down at a table and looking about him, playing with his ponytail in the way that he had taken to doing recently.

We followed in more nervously, scuttling, heads down, to join him.

Bill was fixing some hamburgers while his daughter, who was eighteen and almost as big as her dad, came over to take our order. We had been there five minutes before he noticed us.

He walked over, drying his mighty hands on a tea cloth. As he approached, Sam murmured, 'Leave this to me, fellas.'

'I thought I'd told you three,' said Burger Bill. 'When I say you're banned, you are banned.'

'Excuse me, sir.' Sam's voice was a timid squeak. 'Yeah?'

'I know that these boys have been in a little trouble in the past, but it wasn't their fault, sir.' Sam frowned, as if troubled by a painful memory. 'It was my brother, the boy who was with them.'

'Spare me the fairy tales,' said Bill. 'Hop it, the lot of you.'

'He's gone back to America now,' Sam said quickly. 'He's in a foster home. They said he was' – he sniffed dramatically – 'disturbed.'

Burger Bill crossed his arms. 'Oh yeah?'

'Ever since my mum died in a car crash...' Sam's voice cracked. 'Simon's been running wild. Staying over with our cousins in London, every day, every night, we had only one thing on our minds. Mom.'

'Mum, car crash.' Bill shook his head. 'You kids'll do anything, won't you?'

And suddenly, to our amazement – to our horror – Sam's eyes filled with tears. He stared sightlessly beyond where Jake and I were sitting, as if, at that very moment, he was seeing the crash that really had killed his mother. Then, making no attempt to hide his face, he closed his eyes. There were no sobs, no sounds at all, but tears, more tears than seemed humanly possible, ran down his cheeks and splashed on to the Formica table.

A father who was sitting with a couple of little girls at a nearby table, looked over, concerned.

Burger Bill glanced across at me. 'It's true?' he asked quietly.

I nodded.

Shaking his head, as if having to deal with children whose mothers had been killed was just another thing sent to make his life more difficult, he wandered back to the counter.

Sam sat immobile, eyes closed, tears still flowing. When Tyrone laid a hand on his shoulder, he took a deep breath, then wiped his eyes and his nose with the back of his sleeve. 'I guess we're staying, right?' he muttered.

Sure, we were staying, but frankly it wasn't the greatest party of all time. Bill's daughter brought us burgers with French fries, but none of us felt like talking now. I noticed that Sam, who normally ate everything, left most of his food.

We prepared to pay. Burger Bill walked over to where we sat. 'Don't worry about that,' he said in a low voice so that none of the customers could hear him. 'It's on the house just this once.'

We muttered our thanks. Bill hovered near the table as we stood up.

'Um, miss,' he said to Sam. 'I'm really sorry about your mother and all that.'

Sam nodded and pushed his way out through the glass door on to the shopping precinct.

Burger Bill

I don't blame myself. When kids come into my place and behave like bloomin' yahoos, it's my job to put them straight. There was no way I could have known that the long-haired American boy who had caused the fight was upset by the death of his mother.

But I was glad that his sister had put me straight. She was a sweet little thing and what she told me broke my heart for a whole afternoon.

I'm a parent myself, so I understand these things.

Tyrone

We walked out of the precinct to a busy street. The sun was shining brightly and probably for the last time before autumn closed in, an ice-cream van was parked on a side street near by.

Matt suggested that, since we had just saved some money, we should treat ourselves to a cornet. Still a bit down after what had happened at Burger Bill's, we joined the queue.

Sam was at the back. At the moment when Jake was being served, he said, in a quiet, disbelieving voice, the single word, 'No.'

Matt and I looked at him. He was gazing across the street where a bright-blue car – one of those really small ones – had parked. On this side, a woman with B-movie blonde hair and wearing jeans so tight they looked as if they had been sprayed on, was leaning on the roof of the car.

On the pavement beyond her, a short, bald guy, dressed in a sharp black suit and wearing dark glasses, was talking to a group of people. From the way they were looking down the street and pointing, it seemed as if the man was being given directions.

'It can't be.' Sam's face was deathly white. He walked towards the couple.

'Sam,' I called out. When he kept going, I followed.

He went down the street, twenty metres or so, then we both crossed over. He began walking briskly towards where the blue car was parked.

As we approached, Sam slowed his pace to take a closer look at the man. I was less interested in his face than in his voice. He spoke loudly in an American accent.

After we had passed, Sam pretended to look into the window of an electrical store. His eyes reflected back at me in the glass. They were dark and wide, but the look on his face was empty of any expression.

'D'you know that man?' I asked.

He nodded slowly. 'It's my dad,' he said.

12

Ottoleen

Here's a thing about people in Britain. They say 'yes' when they mean 'no'. In the States, if you ask someone the way to a street they've never heard of, they just shake their heads and keep walking.

Here they stop. 'Somerton Gardens,' they say slowly. 'Yes, now where is that?' It takes five minutes for them to admit that they ain't got a clue.

I see this real quick, but Crash has this old-fashioned thing about believing people. So it takes about fifteen minutes, with people walking by, staring at us like we're unusual or something, before Crash gets any notion as to where we're going.

'What a country.' Crash squeezes himself into the Nissan, sweat soaking through his best red shirt. He crunches the car into gear and we're gone.

Matthew

I could tell from the way Tyrone looked as they crossed the street on their way back to us that something bad had happened. He was walking close to Sam and just behind him, almost as if he thought my cousin might throw himself under the wheels of a car at any moment

Then I looked at Sam. He was always pale, but now he was sheet white. The way he looked, blank and empty, reminded me of how he was that day – years ago, it now seemed – when he turned up on my doorstep beside my mum.

They walked up to us.

'What's happened?' Jake asked.

Tyrone shot him a warning look. 'Sam thinks he's seen his dad,' he said.

'I don't think,' said Sam in a hard, cold voice. 'I know.'

'Here?' I said. 'In London?'

'He was the guy in the blue car,' said Tyrone.

'That was your father?' I could sense that Jake was trying to square the man we had seen – a pudgy little bald guy dressed up like something out of a gangster movie – with the heroic hard man Sam had talked about in the past. 'He's...different from how I had imagined.'

'Yeah?' said Sam in a flat monotone: 'Seems like the same old Crash to me – except he's got himself a new girlfriend.'

'But why's he in London?' asked Jake.

Sam was looking down the road in the direction the small blue car had taken. 'He ain't here to see the sights, that's for sure,' he said.

After Jake and Tyrone said goodbye and left us on the High Street, we made our way towards the park.

'All that stuff about your father being in jail,' I said, breaking the silence as we went. 'Was it true?'

Sam nodded. 'Sure, it was true.'

'You acted like you were...proud of him,' I said carefully.

Sam seemed to think about this for a while. 'I guess you can be proud of someone and still not want to see them too much.'

'Can you?'

A sort of wince, a flicker of pain, crossed Sam's face and, for a moment, I thought he was going to tell me what this was all about. 'It's complicated,' he said.

'We'd better tell my parents,' I said as I walked.

Sam looked across and gave me the benefit of one of his smiles, 'Maybe I'll leave that one up to you, cuz,' he said.

Mr Burton

I was at my desk in the sitting room, catching up on some much-delayed paperwork, when I heard the boys come home. There were mutterings in the hall and the sound of one of them going upstairs.

Moments later, Matthew opened the door. From the look on his face, I could see that something – probably something bad – had happened.

'Sam's just seen his father,' he said.

'Ah.' I made a note in the margin of my proofs to remind me where I was and put the papers on one side of the desk. 'So Mr Lopez is in town.'

'You don't seem surprised.'

'Take a seat, Matthew,' I said. 'I think that maybe it's time to bring you up to date on one or two background developments.'

And out it came – the call from Durkowitz, the story of Sam's inheritance, the distinct possibility that his jailbird father might be taking an interest in the situation. By the time I had finished, Matthew was shaking his head.

'So much for our family not keeping secrets,' he said.

'Under normal circumstances, we would have told you both about what was going on, but' – I hesitated, choosing my words carefully – 'your mother and I thought it would be better if Sam settled into his new school before we worried him further. It was a question of timing.'

'So Lopez is here for the money, you think.'

'From what Gail told your mother, he was never the most conscientious of fathers.'

'Sam was pretty shocked to see him. It's strange – he's always talking about his father but, from the way he's acting, I don't think he's too crazy about the idea of going home with him.'

'Which, of course, is a problem,' I said. 'Not many courts of law would agree to keep a son away from his own father.'

'Sam's not ready to make up his mind,' said Matthew. 'We need to keep him out of sight for a while.'

'Listen, Matthew.' I smiled reassuringly. 'The important thing now is that this is a grown-up problem which we shall solve in the best way for all concerned. Leave it to us and—'

'No.' Matthew interrupted me and spoke with a startling firmness in his voice. 'It's not a grown-up problem,' he said. 'It's a Sam problem. I'll talk to him.'

I was about to suggest that we might wait for Mary to return and hold a family conference, but before I could speak, Matthew was gone.

Matthew

Sam was sitting on his bed, staring into space.

I sat down on the side of the bed and said, in as cool and matter-of-fact a tone as I could manage, 'It turns out that one or two things have been happening without our knowing.'

'Yeah?' Sam's voice was distant, bored.

I told him about the money, the wealth that was his, the cash that would keep flowing in, so long as the records of a group called 666 kept on selling. Normally I'd have expected him to cheer up at this point – Sam has always had a deep affection and respect for the dollar – but now he just sighed, as if none of it mattered any more.

'So Mom wasn't quite so dumb,' he said quietly. We were reaching the tricky bit in our conversation, but Sam was there first. 'My dad knows about this, right?' I nodded. 'And that's why he's flown over to London. Not to see me, but to get his hands on the cash.'

'Maybe,' I said. 'Maybe not.'

'More than maybe. I know the guy.'

I looked at him for a moment. There was something helpless about Sam at times like this. All his swagger and bounce seemed to fall away, leaving this pale, solemn kid, as lost and lonely as anyone could be.

'Was he really such a terrible father?' I asked.

To my surprise, Sam shook his head. 'He wasn't so bad. Sure he and Mom had these big fights and he hung out with other women and he was always in some kind of trouble with the cops, but he had his good points.'

'Like?'

'As I got older, we spent more time together. We went out, just him, his guys and me. He' – an odd smile had appeared on Sam's face – 'involved me in his work, shall we say.'

I waited, sensing there was more to come.

'A kid can be useful,' Sam murmured. 'Say, when you're cashing a stolen cheque and you've got a four-year-old creating all kinds of mayhem, it can make the cashier want to hand over the money just to get you out of there. Or when you need to get past the security guard in an office building, it helps if you've got junior in tow, bawling that he needs to go to the bathroom. Or if there's some little guy, acting like he's lost and frightened on the sidewalk, it can distract the cops for a few minutes. Stuff like that.'

I tried not to look shocked. 'He took you on jobs with him?'

'He introduced me to the family business a bit earlier than is usual. It was all right until...' Sam looked down and flicked the thumb of his right hand as if tossing an invisible coin. 'Until we kind of hit a wall.'

'A wall?'

Sam turned to look at me. 'If he takes me back, I'll be gone. I'd take a hike. Hang out with a few of my old buddies from the gang.'

'You'd run away?'

'Sam Lopez does not run away. He relocates.'

I thought for a moment. 'So you don't want your father to find you for a while.'

'That would seem to be the case.'

I told him my plan. Even before I had finished he was laughing.

Mr Burton

Mary had returned from work and we were in the kitchen, discussing the latest developments, when Matthew re-appeared.

He told us that he had talked the whole thing through with Sam, that he had told him about the inheritance left by Gail. He said they had come up with a possible solution. 'It might be a bit of a surprise,' he said. 'Just keep an open mind.'

To be frank, we were already in shock. This was not the Matthew we knew. The Sam crisis had changed him. We were used to a child – funny, awkward, our little boy. Suddenly it was as if he were taking charge not only of his cousin but of us, his parents.

I tried, as kindly as possible, to point out that, although we were grateful for his help, we had decided that it was impossible and impractical to keep Sam hidden for any length of time. On balance, we thought it was best to ask the advice of the police. 'This is serious stuff,' I said. By all accounts this Mr Lopez is not the most savoury of characters.'

It was at this point that the door behind me opened. Mary, who was sitting opposite me, looked over my shoulder.

Then she screamed.

Mrs Burton

As it happens, I probably haven't allowed one involuntary sound of any volume to escape from my lips since I was about eleven years old.

But when I looked up to see her...him...it, standing there at the kitchen door, I felt a genuine sense of shock – even of fear.

It was a girl. Yet it wasn't a girl. It was Sam. I could see that. All the same, he was so perfectly self-contained, so completely undisguised, that it just took my breath away. It was as if we were not seeing a fake, female version of Sam but that this was the real thing.

'Hi, folks,' he said quietly.

'Bloody hell,' said David.

Solemnly, Sam walked past us to the far wall, then turned, ambled back, and sat on one of the chairs. 'Welcome to the new me,' he said.

'Where did you get the clothes?' asked David.

'They were Jake's sister's,' said Matthew. 'We borrowed them.'

'Well.' David tried for a smile but managed a wince. 'You certainly look at home in them.'

'That's because I've been wearing them all week,' said Sam.

'What?' This was both David and me.

Matthew smiled. 'We had this idea. It was sort of a challenge. We wanted to trick the girls in class.'

'I've never heard anything so thoroughly irresponsible in all my life,' I said. 'Did it work?'

'What do you think?' Sam widened his eyes slightly and smiled in an alarmingly feminine manner.

'So that explains the plucked eyebrows,' said David. 'And you must have been Simone, Matthew's girlfriend.'

'Please don't think I was too happy about that.'

I was looking more closely at him now and noticed something for the first time. 'Sam, are those breasts?' I asked.

Crash

We cruised by, late that night, checking out 23 Somerton Gardens, the crock of gold at the end of the rainbow. Inside there were lights, people moving about, just like any family, all innocent and unaware that sharks were circling their little pool.

'I can almost smell the money,' I said.

'Miew' went Ottoleen. She was one happy kitten that night.

Matthew

Now here's a surprise. My parents were none too hot on the idea of Sam becoming a girl, round the clock, until his father gave up and went home. They came up with one objection after another – practical, legal, whether it would be a bad, bad thing that we would be doing – but the more we talked, the clearer the position became. This was one tough project – the stakes were high and so were the risks.

But if we all played our part, we could carry it off. Whether it was worth it or not came down to one person.

Late that evening, after supper, we sat in the living room and the silences grew longer and longer.

'Maybe we should just be honest and straightforward and take it to the courts,' Dad said.

'We would simply explain that Sam has settled into life here,' said my mother. 'Mr Lopez would be very welcome to visit now and then.'

But Sam was shaking his head. 'You don't get it, you guys,' he said softly. 'Crash just doesn't do honest and straightforward. The only time he's been in a court is when his lawyer lets him take the stand. He'll get me back – somehow he'll do it.'

'How would you feel about that?' Mum asked.

Sam gazed at her for a moment, a cold and stony stare.

'More to the point is, how would you feel, Mrs Burton?'

My mother held his look, then smiled. 'I would be very sad, Sam Lopez.'

'Me too,' said Dad.

All three looked at me. 'Yeah.' I shrugged. 'I admit it would be pretty boring without you around. It's almost like you're part of the family.'

Sam blinked rapidly as if some speck of dirt was in his eye, then seemed to notice something on the floor which required his close attention. 'I guess...' He frowned. 'I guess that's how I feel too.'

Mum made as if to put an arm around Sam's shoulders, but he shrank back, holding up his hands in mock horror. 'Easy,' he said. 'One step at a time, right?'

There was a moment of silence as each of us came to terms with the big scene of family bonding that had just taken place.

'We need to work out what to do next,' said my father eventually. 'Tomorrow's Friday. Go to school as' – he smiled – 'normal. We'll make a decision over the weekend.'

Sam shrugged and stood up. 'Suits me,' he said. 'But when he finds out where you live, old Crash'll come knocking soon enough.'

'Why do they call him Crash?' Mum asked.

'You'll find out,' said Sam.

13

Elena

Like all Libras, I'm totally sensitive to other people's mood swings, so when Sam came in the next day looking all washed out and weary, I just knew that something important had happened to her.

It was time to prove that I was her real friend. She might have a whole two-little-songbirds thing going with my ex-friend, Zia Khan, but when it came down to real life, there was nothing to beat the old El and Sam Show.

I managed to catch her alone after the first lesson. I was, 'All right, Sammo?'

'Sure,' she said. 'Why not?'

'I just wanted to say that I'm here for you. If you want to talk something through, I'm a really good listener. It's what friends are for.'

'Thanks,' she said. 'I just feel kind of out of it today – a little spacey, you know?'

I knew all right. My instinct had been on the money as usual. 'I think you'll find that your problem lies in three little letters,' I said. Then I whispered them in her ear.

'What?' said Sam.

'Don't worry,' I said. 'I'll leave something in your locker, just in case. It's important to be prepared.'

'But...what exactly is PMT?' she asked.

'You must know.' I laughed. 'Premenstrual tension. You'll find that, just before you get your period, you'll get really short-tempered and snappy. It's nothing to be embarrassed about – a lot of girls have it.'

'Yeah?' said Sam. 'That explains a lot.'

I laughed. 'I won't tell a soul,' I said.

Charley

Sam had started. Elena was the first person to twig. She confided in Kate and Donna. Soon every girl in Year Eight was passing on the day's hot gossip.

Sam had started.

When Steve asked her a question in English and she just went on staring into space, there were significant glances all round.

When she ate hardly any lunch, Elena mouthed the word 'Cramps' in my direction.

All in all, it was the day's hot news.

Mark

I had it bad. It was like a fever, an illness that took over my brain and body. I couldn't concentrate in class – nothing new there, but the guys in my gang started taking the mick out of me. They nudged one another and made moony faces when I passed. My cool was slipping. My rep was in serious jeopardy.

But the American babe showed no sign of thawing out.

When I sauntered up to her that Friday afternoon, said, 'Hi, Sam,' and gave her the full-on Kramer smile, she looked at me slowly, as if coming out of a dream. 'Made a decision yet?'

'Decision?' she said.

'About going out.'

'Going out? What you talking about, man?'

'A club? Or maybe a gig. I've heard you like music. We could take in some girl band somewhere.'

Sam shook her lovely head as if she had more important things to think about than dating Mark Kramer.

'She's not in the mood, Mark,' said one of her friends, Charley Johnson.

'I could handle going to a club with you if you want,' the Elena creature chirped up.

I ignored her and stepped closer to Sam. It was time for the Kramer voice, low and silky. That always does the trick.

'How about it, Sam?' I murmured. 'It's Friday. Face it, everyone's in the mood on Friday.'

'If you must know.' This was the skinny little oddball Elena again. 'She has female troubles. If you don't know what those are, ask your mum.'

'Female troubles?' I laughed. 'There are no female troubles that a good, strong dose of Mark Kramer can't cure.'

Sam Lopez seemed to tune into the conversation at this point. She reached into her jacket pocket. 'Yeah,

El's right,' she said. 'I've got female troubles.' She took out what looked very like one of those tampon things that girls have. She poked my chest with it, hard. 'Get it now, doughbrain? I'm having a very...heavy...day.'

'OK, OK.' I raised two hands in surrender and backed off. 'Maybe some other time then.'

Elena

We had shared a bra. And we had shared my supply of tampons. No one could say that I wasn't Sam's best friend now.

All the same, I was the teeniest bit surprised by the way she talked to Mark that afternoon – and frankly, I hadn't left a packet of Tampax in her locker for it to be used as an offensive weapon!

But then we can all be a bit moody at that time of the month, can't we?

Matthew

Sam and I walked home in silence.

Eventually I asked the big question. 'What's it going to be then? Boy or girl?'

Sam shrugged. 'Search me,' he said.

He took longer than usual to change back into his normal clothes that evening.

Ottoleen

When Crash is preparing to make a move he becomes very still, like a panther just about to pounce on a deer or whatever. (I admit that Crash doesn't look like a panther, he's a bit wider than a panther and has got less fur than a panther and a panther doesn't click its knuckles when it's nervous, but you know what I mean.) I keep myself to myself when he's like this.

That day we stayed in the hotel, except for when we went out to McDonald's in the middle of the day.

Chewing on a Big Mac, he told me that he had this plan to pay a little visit to Mr and Mrs Burton sometime in the early evening.

'That's when the kids are going to be around, right?' I said.

'Nah,' he said. 'That's when folk have their TVs on. Drowns out the screamin'.'

I wasn't crazy about this screaming thing. 'I thought we were just going to check that little Sam was there,' I said.

'Drowns out the screamin'.' He repeated the words, just like I hadn't said anything.

Crash was ready all right.

Mrs Burton

It was just after seven when we heard the ring at the door. There was something about that ring – the way it lasted about ten seconds longer than is generally considered polite – that told me that it was the famous Mr Lopez.

I was feeling perfectly confident – this is my home, for heaven's sake – but I noticed that David was looking a bit peaky. I told the boys to go upstairs and went to open the front door.

Crash

Inside I was wired, twitching like a finger on the trigger of a gun. Outside I was a smiling, innocent American visitor, a family man looking for his son.

I wore a suit and a white shirt and a tie that was tight against my neck. And Ottoleen? That afternoon she had shown me what she planned to wear, the skin-tight jeans and clinging T-shirt.

'Too hot,' I said.

She tried the short black skirt.

'Way too hot.'

We went shopping and got some English floral thing, and bought it a couple of sizes bigger than she likes to wear. 'We all have to make sacrifices,' I said.

So there we were, on the doorstep. Mr and Mrs Straight-'n'-Respectable.

A tall woman opened the front door. 'Hello,' she said, a fixed kiss-off smile on her face.

'Mrs Burton?' I said.

'Yes.'

'My name is Anthony Lopez,' I said. 'I was married to your late sister, Galaxy.'

'Oh,' she said. 'What a nice surprise.'

'This is my wife, Mrs Lopez.'

'Pleased to meet you,' said Ottoleen, with a polite, little-girl smile. '

'How do you do?' said Mrs Burton.

'Very well,' said Ottoleen.

We stood there for a couple of beats. Then the Burton woman said, 'You'd better come in.'

We stepped into the hall, which was done up in a dingy English style with flower pictures on the wall and lighting like it's out of some 1950s film.

'Nice place you got here, Mrs Burton,' said Ottoleen.

The woman seemed not to hear and walked ahead of us. Throwing Ottoleen a quick wink, I followed her into a sitting room where Mr Burton, a suburban sort of guy who was actually wearing a cardigan, sat reading a newspaper.

More introductions. We took our places on a sofa, Ottoleen managing to show more leg than was strictly appropriate for the occasion.

Mr Burton offered us a drink.

'I don't,' I said.

'A cup of tea would be nice,' said Ottoleen.

To my surprise it was the guy who got up to make it in the kitchen.

We made small talk, all sad and sorrowful, about the late Galaxy, with me giving a little speech about how she was quite a character, they broke the mould when they made her, big loss to us all, et cetera, et cetera. 'One of the greatest regrets of my life', I said, 'was that I was away on a business trip and only heard of her tragic demise after the funeral.'

When Mr Burton returned with a tray and poured out some tea, I cut to the chase.

'I was informed that you have been looking after my boy, Sam,' I said.

'Your son?' Mrs Burton gazed at me coolly over the rim of her teacup. 'But he's in a foster home, isn't he?'

I smiled to cover my surprise. 'I don't think so. You came to the funeral and you took him away. Now I want him back.'

'Do you know, I think there's been a terrible misunderstanding,' said Mrs Burton, giving me the big freeze. 'I certainly attended my sister's funeral but I returned alone.'

'Misunderstanding?' I said. 'You're kidding me?'

'No, I'm not...kidding you, Mr Lopez. I suggest that you direct your enquiries through the correct legal channels.'

I felt a tight knot of rage forming in the pit of my stomach.

Ottoleen

Beside me I feel Crash tense up as if he's trying to keep his cool. I murmur 'Crash' but it's too late. He brings down the hand that's holding his teacup hard, and there's bits of china and tea all over the table, scattering across the carpet.

'He's my son!' he shouts.

Mr and Mrs Burton are looking kind of wide-eyed and freaked now, but they say nothing.

'It's the money, isn't it,' goes Crash. 'You're holding

out to cut some kind of deal, but listen, maybe you don't understand what you're dealing with here. This is family, right? This is family money. That means it's sacred.'

Mr Burton is staring down at the broken china and looks like he's going to do a you-know-what in his pants, but Mrs Burton kind of squares her shoulders.

'I have absolutely no idea what you're talking about,' she says.

Crash

I got to my feet and the Burton guy flinched like I was about to pull a piece on him.

'You want to do this the hard way?' I said. 'Then be my guest.'

I left the room, looked in the kitchen. Then I ran upstairs, two steps at a time.

There were three closed doors. I pushed away into the first room – a big bedroom, empty. In the second, some kid was sitting in front of a computer. He started when I opened the door.

'Where's Sam?' I asked.

'Who?' he said.

There was music from behind the third closed door. I pushed it open.

And there was this blonde kid, brushing her hair in front of a mirror. She looked up at me coolly. 'Can I help you?' she asked.

'Who are you?' I asked.

'I'm Simone,' she said. 'Who are you?'

Ottoleen

Crash has cooled down somewhat by the time he re-appears in the sitting room.

'There are two kids upstairs,' he speaks to me as if the Burtons aren't there. 'But no Sam.'

'Two?' I go.

'Yeah, a British kid and someone called Simone.'

Mrs Burton actually smiles at this point. 'Ah, yes, Simone is a friend from Canada,' she says. 'She's over here on an exchange programme.'

Mr Burton stands up and says, 'I'm so sorry that you've had a wasted journey.'

Crash tells him that he can get you-know-whated for all he cares and storms out of the house.

I go, 'Thank you for the tea,' and follow.

This is not what we planned.

Matthew

Slam. That was the front door. Slam, slam. Two car doors. Then the revving of an engine, a squeal of tyres. Then silence.

I made my way to Sam's room. He was sitting on the bed in his coat and skirt. Ten minutes ago, when we had come upstairs, he had been Sam, the guy. While the adults were talking downstairs, he must have changed.

'So that was your dad.'

He was staring ahead of him. 'Yup,' he said quietly.

'You made up your mind then?'

He nodded.

My parents appeared behind me.

'Well done, Sam,' said my mother, her voice shaky as if she was still in shock. 'You were very brave.'

My father sat down on the bed and put an arm around Sam's shoulder. 'Are you all right?' he asked.

Sam shrugged him off, a look of real distaste on his face. 'Just leave me alone,' he said.

Dad stood up and the three of us waited uncertainly in Sam's small room.

'Bug off, all of you,' he said in a quiet, weary voice.

Tyrone

Matt messaged me the news that night. CRASH VISITED SAM NOW BOY2GIRL FULL-TIME, he wrote.

Any other time, I would have wanted to know more, but the truth was, that night I had my own problems.

After school, my mother took me round to Juliana's house where I met the girl she's determined I should go out with.

Let me put this as kindly as I can. She was not exactly my type – skinny, taller than me and with a face like a sour plum. After tea, Mrs Lavery offered to show my mother some new curtains upstairs (yeah, right), leaving me with Juliana.

It was the longest and most embarrassing five minutes of my life. I didn't like Juliana. Juliana was not too impressed with me. We had nothing in common. We ran out of conversation after about thirty seconds and, having sat in silence for about a minute, Juliana skipped (I hate skippers) to the piano and started plonking away.

When eventually the parents returned, they looked at us – her at the piano, me on the sofa – and smiled as if they were witnessing the most romantic thing they had ever seen.

'So,' said Mum when at last we got out of there. 'What do you think?'

'No,' I said. 'That's what I think. No, no, no.'

My mother smiled in a sickeningly knowing way. 'These things take time,' she said.

14

Matthew

I'll say this much for Sam. Once he made up his mind, there was no shifting him.

That Saturday morning, he came down to breakfast in his school uniform, as if being a girl were the most natural thing in the world.

'So when we going shopping?' he asked my mother.

'Shopping?'

'And I don't want no low-class tat,' he said. 'Simone likes to accessorise, right?'

Mum frowned. 'I'll give you a hundred pounds. That's quite enough for you boys to get a nice dress, a blouse and some shoes.'

'A hundred and fifty pounds,' said Sam. 'I want a bag too. Maybe some make-up.'

'You're far too young for that,' said Mum.

'A hundred and fifty pounds, please,' said Sam.

Defeated, my mother reached for her handbag. 'I think I preferred you as a boy,' she said.

Zia

I spent the weekend in my room, writing songs. Hearing Sam sing had released something in me. Suddenly I knew the sound that I wanted from my music. On the surface, it would be bouncy, acoustic, guitar-band stuff, but underneath there would be some weird chords, all minors and diminished sevenths and stuff, just when you were least expecting them.

In my head, I could hear Sam's voice, high and pure but with an edge to it, a sort of strange, mysterious sadness. It may sound stupid, but I knew that, with my songs and backing vocals and Sam's voice, something special would emerge.

I wrote about being alone, about wanting a boyfriend, about feeling different from other people, about someone who was so into herself that she was hardly able to see straight (take a bow, Elena Griffiths). They weren't exactly songs to make you glad to feel alive – in fact, most of them were downright doomy – but they were better than anything I had written before.

By the end of the weekend, I had written five new songs, 'Inside My Room', 'Mr Perfect', 'Private Cloud', 'Invisible' and 'The Ego Has Landed'. I played the guitar and vocals into the tape machine in my room and typed out the lyrics on my dad's laptop.

Sam was in for a big surprise on Monday.

Jake

You know how it is when someone tells a joke and it goes on just that bit too long? The smile muscles begin to ache, right? You want to say, 'OK, we got it. Can we move on now?'

That's how it as on the Saturday when Tyrone, Matt and me hit the High Street with the official Miss Sam Lopez.

It had seemed such a good idea, shaking up the girls by sneaking a spy into their midst. Now it was no longer about Elena and her crew. Sam was getting kitted out for girlhood, and none of us knew how long it would be before he became a boy again.

Another reason why the joke had suddenly got serious: old Crash-Bang-Wallop was in town. From what Matt said, he was like the Godfather meets the Terminator. Now, if Sam got caught, his whole life would change.

So that Saturday, the day it all changed, Sam was different. He still played the part of a girl, prancing about, trying on his clothes, giving the shop assistants hell, but now and then there was a look in his eye – a hard, unforgiving glint – that reminded me of the way he was when he first arrived.

We were at Burger Bill's, a favourite since Sam had convinced him that he was Little, Miss Tragedy. Shopping bags were around our feet, and, thanks to the cash Sam now had, we were each tucking into Bill's Burger de Luxe, the most expensive item on the menu.

'So how do I look?' Sam asked at one point.

We looked at him. The hair was in a ponytail, he

had dangly silver earrings in the shape of his star sign, Scorpio, some coloured false nails. He was wearing a tank top and there was a pale stomach showing above green trousers.

'All right,' said Matt. 'But my mum's not going to like those nails. They're way too tarty.'

Sam was looking at his reflection in the window. 'I had never seen myself as a tank-top girl, but there you go,' he said. 'You don't know if something's going to suit you until you put it on.'

I caught Matt's eye and he gave a slight wince. Sam, the fashion victim – it was all we needed.

'You don't think you're getting into this a bit too much?' I said to Sam, as casually as I could.

Sam gave me a look which reminded me of our big fight at this very table during the summer holiday: 'How d'you mean?' he said.

I noticed that Tyrone and Matt were giving me don't-go-there looks, but I decided to ignore them. 'The clothes, the act, the voice. They're all very well, but don't you wish you could be normal?'

'What's normal?' said Sam.

I laughed. 'Not dressing up as a girl maybe.'

Sam clenched his fist, but then seemed to relax. He stretched out his fingers and examined his fake nails. 'It's different being a girl. You can do things you can't do as a guy. It's kinda fun sometimes. You got a problem with that, old boy?'

I looked at him more closely. The strip lighting had revealed something about Sam that I had failed to notice before.

'Not as big a problem as you have,' I said. With one finger, I tapped his upper lip. 'Nice little moustache you're growing there, old girl.'

Sam put a hand to his mouth. Muttering, 'No need to get personal,' he stood up and wandered over to the cash desk. 'I'll pay for them all, Mr Bill,' he said.

'That doesn't seem right.' Burger Bill winked at the three of us as we approached. 'You boys allowing the little lady to pick up the tab?'

Sam pulled a roll of notes from his back pocket and peeled off a twenty-pound note.

'We don't talk about little ladies any more, Mr Bill,' he said. 'It's what we call sexism.'

Bill seemed about to say something, but then, perhaps remembering that the American girl had problems in her life, he thought better of it and pushed the change back across the counter with a curt, 'There you go, love.'

Tyrone

It was when we were at Burger Bill's, with Jake just asking to get his face smashed but somehow getting away with it, that a rather brilliant little idea occurred to me.

As we made our way through the precinct, I mentioned it to Sam.

To my amazement and joy, he agreed.

Ottoleen

That weekend Crash is totally stir-crazy. He keeps saying, 'If Sam isn't with the you-know-what Burtons, where the you-know-what is he?'

We talk about whether the stuck-up English family we visited might have hidden him away somewhere, but then we figure they couldn't have known we were going to turn up on their doorstep. He puts in some calls to his contacts in America. They tell him that the word is that the kid's still in London.

So Crash mulls all this over, gazing out of the window, chewing gum, looking at the grey London scene.

It's then that I have my great idea. 'How about if we call up some schools?'

'Turn the volume up on some of the teachers?' goes Crash. 'I guess it could work.'

'What I mean is that maybe the kid's been shipped off to another family in the area, so we can't track him down. But he still has to go to school, doesn't he?'

Crash is cracking his knuckles. 'Maybe we could bust into the principal's office, grab the pupil list and—'

'Which school, Crash?'

He frowns and thinks about this for a moment. 'You got a point there, babe,' he says.

I open the drawer to the bedside table, take out a local telephone directory and look up the listing for schools in the area.

I pick up the phone and dial. 'Is that St Peters?' I ask in my best, butter-wouldn't-melt voice. 'Ah, thank you very much. I'm a parent and I've just moved into the area.

Your school was recommended to me by one of my son's friends, Sam Lopez...You don't have a Sam Lopez? Sorry to trouble you, ma'am.'

When I hang up, Crash is giving me the look I know so well, the one that's telling me I don't know you-know-what about detective work.

Just this once, I decide to ignore him. I dial the next number.

Mrs O'Grady

Being a successful school, Bradbury Hill gets all sorts of enquiries from would-be parents coming through to the school office, but, as it happens, I do recall receiving an enquiry from a lady with an American accent.

When she mentioned the name of Sam Lopez, I was tempted to tell her that having one troublesome American in the school was quite enough, but, at the end of the day, I am professional enough to know that it's my boss, Mrs Cartwright, who must make these decisions.

'I'm delighted that Sam has recommended us,' I said in my coolest voice. 'But we require all applications for entry to the school to be made in writing.'

Crash

Like all women, Ottoleen gets these crazy ideas in her head. I guess that simply by the law of averages one of them had to be OK.

I had dozed off on the bed, the sound of my wife making these calls, one after another, in the background, when suddenly I was woken by this mad whoop of triumph.

I opened my eyes. She was standing at the end of the bed with this piece of paper in her hand.

'Now what?' I said.

'I found it,' she says, a big smile all over her face. 'I found out where your boy is.'

I took the paper and read the name that was written down in her loopy handwriting.

'Bradbury Hill Secondary School.' I smiled. 'You know, for a broad, you can be pretty smart sometimes.'

'Why, thank you, Crash,' she said.

Mrs Sherman

Tyrone and I have a very good relationship. Very open, you know? When something is on his mind, he knows he can talk to his old mum about it. And if I'm a bit concerned about, say, the amount of time he spends with his rather uncouth, scruffy, inarticulate, under-achieving two male friends, I can share my thoughts with him in a caring, motherly way.

'And they speak very highly of you too, Mum,' he'll say (he's very quick, my son – I think he could be a politician one day).

So when, over breakfast on that first Sunday after the beginning of term, Tyrone mentioned that he had a friend coming round for tea, I was able to joke, 'One of your Neanderthal "mates", I suppose.'

Tyrone bit into his toast. 'Not that Neanderthal, as it happens,' he said, chewing.

'Sitting in front of your laptop, making occasional grunting noises at one another. Honestly, you boys.'

'She's not a boy, actually,' said Tyrone, cool as you like. 'And she doesn't grunt.'

'She?' I remember that my teacup was halfway to my mouth when this momentous news struck home. 'Did you say "she"?'

'Yup.'

'It's not Juliana, is it?' I asked hopefully. Tyrone made a vulgar puking gesture. 'So who is it?' I asked.

'You'll see.'

'Are you telling me you've got a girlfriend, Tyrone?'

He seemed to think about this for a moment. 'Let's say we're just good friends at the moment. I don't want to crowd her – you know how it is.'

'I do know, of course I do. Maybe I should get crumpets for tea. Chestnuts! We could roast chestnuts on the fire and—'

'Mum.' Tyrone gave me the weary look which he does so well.

'You don't want me around, do you? You're ashamed of your own mother.'

'No. I'd like you to meet her. Just cool it with the old happy-family-round-the-fire thing. She's a bit shy.'

'Fine,' I said. 'That's just fine.'

Tyrone

So that was my idea. We had helped Sam. Now it was time for Sam to help me.

It was going to be a piece of cake.

Mrs Sherman

What do you wear for a visit from your son's first girl-friend? I know parents are expected to know this kind of thing by instinct, but I have always found it rather difficult. After several false starts, I opted for a relaxed but formal trouser suit, but wore some purple designer trainers to show that I am an easy-going, young-at-heart sort of mum.

As it turned out, I needn't have worried. When she appeared, Sam, as I learned her name to be, was a charming little thing – not at all like some of the bossy, loud-mouthed girls one sees around town.

As we sipped our tea in the conservatory, Tyrone went into silent-male mode as I tried to make Sam feel at home.

She was American, which I thought was a good thing. I've always found Americans to be rather more dynamic and ambitious than Europeans.

'Do you have any idea what you might do when you grow up?' I asked Sam at one point.

'I'm going to be a lawyer, ma'am,' she said with the sweetest smile. 'I want to become a partner in a big law firm, and get loads of criminals locked up or maybe even fried in the electric chair, and join the golf club, and make a whole stack of cash and all that stuff.'

'Excellent,' I said. 'I only wish you could persuade Tyrone to be a little more focused about his career.'

Tyrone muttered something inaudible and slouched further down into his chair.

'As it happens, we talk about his career all the time at school,' said Sam.

'You do?' I could hardly believe my ears.

'T says he's thinking of business school,' said Sam. 'I tell him that he should qualify as an accountant first. Then you've got something to build on – qualifications are so important in life aren't they, Mrs Sherman?'

'They are,' I said. I was slightly hurt that my son had not shared these thoughts and plans with me, but delighted that his charming young American girlfriend was such an excellent influence on him.

As if reading my thoughts, Sam chirped up, 'Tyrone likes to pretend he's not serious about his ambitions and that he's just a party guy – a babe-magnet who all the girls want to go out with – but, once you get to know him, you realise there's more to him than just looks.'

Now both Tyrone and I were staring at Sam. Much as I love my boy, I had never exactly seen him in this light. 'Babe-magnet? Isn't he a bit…big for that?',

Sam smiled shyly. 'Fat's the new thin, Mrs Sherman. Flesh is hot, hot, hot. I have to fight the other girls off Tyrone. They call him "T-bone" because there's just so much of him.'

Tyrone was making a low groaning sound. He muttered something through clenched teeth. It sounded like, 'I'm going to kill you, Sam.'

I laughed at this delightful badinage. Then, sensing that the young couple wanted time on their own, I made my excuses and went upstairs.

I was making some calls to other parents – there was no particular reason I needed to talk to them, but I couldn't wait to pass on Tyrone's big news – when I heard raised voices from the drawing room downstairs. The two of them were having a little row. It was a sure sign that they were serious about one another!

Tyrone and Sam. T-bone and his 'babe'. I was terribly proud and happy that day.

Tyrone

That was the thing with Sam. He would help you out but then somehow, in doing so, he could manage to drop you even deeper into the doo-doo.

So, after the visit of my 'girlfriend', there was good news and bad news.

The good news was that my mother stopped thinking of me as some kind of problem kid who would never get a girlfriend or a job. The bad news was that, thanks to Sam, she became the boastful mother from hell. All that evening, she found excuses to ring her friends. From behind the closed doors of her bedroom, tell-tale phrases reached me – 'the sweetest little American girl', 'qualify as an accountant', 'babe-magnet', 'fat's the new thin'.

At last my mother could be proud of me. Gee, thanks a bunch, Sam.

Matthew

Nature can be cruel sometimes. At the very moment when Sam had settled for being a girl while his father was circling around like a hungry vulture, his body started heading in the opposite direction.

That night I explained Sam's moustache problem to my mother. Astonishingly, she volunteered to help us lose it and even happened to have some of the wax stuff which – spare me the details, please, Mum – she now and then had to use herself.

We were in her bedroom. Sam was sitting in front of her dressing-room mirror while this pink stuff dried on his top lip.

'Are you ready to hold him down when I pull it off, Matthew?' Mum joked. 'It hurts.'

'Yeah, right,' said Sam in as tough a voice as a person with pink wax under his nose can manage. 'It's for girls. How bad can that be?'

'All right,' said my mother. 'Don't say I didn't warn you.' She tugged gently at a loose end of the wax.

'Ah!' Sam yelped as the first hairs were plucked from his skin. 'Easy now.'

He shrank back and, at that moment, Mum gave one vicious tug and the moustache came away.

'Agh...agh...aaaagh.' Hand clamped to his mouth, Sam leaped up and did a little dance of pain around the room.

'Told you,' said Mum, looking with some satisfaction at the blond hairs that were on the wax.

'How do girls *do* that?' Sam shouted these words, but it wasn't what he said but how he said it that made Mum and me stare at him in horror. The word 'do' had emerged from his mouth as a cracked, booming, manly bass.

'Uh-oh,' said Mum. 'That's all we need. Now his voice is going to break.'

'No way,' said Sam, a treble once more.

'You'll just have to avoid talking too much,' said my mother.

'Some hope,' I muttered.

15

Steve Forrester

Something odd had happened to Year Eight. The rabble that I remembered from last year, with the few sensible, motivated pupils struggling against a background of disruption, seemed to change. They became almost – how can I put it? – grown-up.

The gender divide between the girls and the boys seemed to narrow. Sometimes I could look up from my desk after the class had been set some work and face the unusual sight of the tops of heads. Normally there would be a few faces staring into space or gazing out of the window or trying to distract one of the other boys (this was essentially a boy problem). Not any more.

When girls answered a question, the boys actually listened. They even put up their hands themselves now and then – and not just to make some foolish remark.

I said nothing about this, not wanting to break the spell, but I couldn't help wondering exactly what was going on. It was like that moment in film westerns when a cowboy says, 'It's quiet – too quiet.'

Elena

Suddenly Zia was coming on like Little Miss Musical Genius. She arrived at school on Monday with the mad, faraway look of someone who has been creating too many wonderful things in her head to have had time to eat, drink, sleep or even go the lavatory.

When Charley asked why we hadn't seen her that weekend, she said she had been 'working on stuff'. Then, when Sam arrived with Matthew and the boys, she practically sprinted over to her, carrying a plastic bag. Charley and I watched as she handed over some sheets of paper, then an old-fashioned tape.

'Get the musical twins,' I said.

'It's good,' said Charley. 'Good for both of them.' But I could tell she was worried.

Mark

I like a challenge. Sometimes, when I'm playing football and the ball is never coming to me or I'm up against some defender who's almost as good as I am, I say to myself, 'OK, Mark Kramer, let's get serious here.' I go into the zone, and soon things begin to happen. A pass, an interception and – bang! – another classic Kramer goal.

That's how it was with the little American, my girlfriend-to-be. I thought about her over the weekend – how I could get her away from her little friends and show her what life could be like with a real man. I went into the zone, the I'm-going-to-get-Sam zone.

That Monday, during lunch break, I ambled up to her when she was chatting to her friends.

'This is for you, Sam,' I said, giving her an envelope.

'What is it?' she asked.

'A ticket for the big game, on Wednesday night. City against United.'

'Whoa,' said Elena. 'Impressive. How did you get that?'

'I've got contacts in the ticket office,' I said, my eyes still on Sam. 'Have we got a date?'

She hesitated, and I could tell that the old Kramer magic was beginning to work on her.

'I'll think about it,' she said. 'I'm not too crazy about soccer, to tell the truth.'

'Don't wait too long, babe. A lot of people would kill for this.' I wandered off coolly, then glanced over my shoulder, ready to give her the old wink, but she had turned away and was talking to her friends.

'She'll come across,' I said to Ben and Jason, a couple of guys from my class who had been watching me.

'You're in a bad way, mate,' said Jason and gave a little pitying laugh.

It was the moment that I knew that this was no longer just between me and Sam Lopez. If she turned me down again, I'd be in trouble. People would start laughing at me.

And Mark Kramer doesn't like that.

Zia

I suppose I had expected Sam to be a bit more excited when I gave her my songs. I had spent all weekend on them, they were good and they were for her.

But there was something strange about Sam that day. She seemed as if she had other things on her mind.

'That's cool,' she said, putting the tape with my songs into her bag. 'I'll listen to them tonight.'

'We could rehearse later in the week,' I said.

'Whatever,' she said.

Then, later that day, when Mark Kramer came over and gave her a ticket for some stupid football game, she seemed really pleased – as if that mattered more to her than my five songs.

Maybe I had got her all wrong. Maybe I'd keep the songs to myself.

Charley

Zed is one of the least moody people I've met, but that day she went into one, big time. When Sam started talking to Elena and me about whether she should go out with Mark Kramer or not, she became really quite upset – surprising because we had all agreed that it was pretty damn great for any of us to be asked out by Mark.

'I do believe she's jealous,' said Elena in her usual tactful way.

'Jealous?' Zia snapped. 'Why should I be jealous of Mark Kramer?'

It took a moment or two for the impact of what she had just said to sink in. El had assumed that she was annoyed because she fancied Mark but, weirdly, it seemed that she wasn't jealous of Sam going out with Mark but of Mark going out with Sam.

'That's not exactly what I meant,' said Elena.

Ottoleen

I'm like suddenly, you know I kinda like it here?

We're at a pub by the Thames river the next day, sitting at one of the outside tables in that watery English sunshine. There are these rowers doing their thing on the grey old river, a young couple with a baby are sitting at a nearby table, and an old guy walks on the path between us and the river and gives this little nod. 'Morning,' he says, like he knows us or something.

'Hi there,' I say.

Crash is staring at the river, his thoughts miles away. 'What?' he says.

'Nothing, hon,' I go. 'I was just saying hello to a walker guy.' I close my eyes and smile. 'This is nice,' I murmur.

'We get the kid and we're gone,' he says, but from the tone of his voice I can tell that he doesn't totally disagree with me.

Away from the States, he's more relaxed. Around here no one knows he's Crash Lopez, entrepreneur, tough guy. He can just be himself. That tense, hard look he wears on his face 24-7 at home, now and then slips into something different here, something almost – I can't believe I'm saying this – mellow. Just now and then I catch a sight of another Crash Lopez – no longer a ball of rage, but a guy who's come to terms with the fact that he's not so young any more, that you don't absolutely have to frighten people just to feel alive.

'So what's the plan, Crash?' I ask.

'I call up the school,' he says. 'We go visit and have a look around for my son.' He sips at his beer and shakes his head like he still can't believe that English pubs don't have fancy cocktails like they do in the States. 'When we find the kid, we need to persuade him to come home of his own accord. We gotta come on like…parents.'

'We'd be good parents,' I say before I can stop myself.

Crash doesn't seem to be listening. He frowns. 'The little fink had better be grateful that we've gone to all this trouble for him.'

'He'll come with us, Crash,' I say. 'You're his father, after all.'

'We used to do stuff together.' Crash gazes out over the Thames. 'Galaxy would rattle on about how I was taking him too fast, how I was treating him more like one of the guys than a son, but that's the Crash Lopez way, right? I didn't know that the kid wasn't up to it.'

I'm about to ask him what exactly Sam wasn't up to, but I can see from Crash's face that he's not in the mood for explanations.

'It was a long time ago,' I say.

'Sure. I guess he's a changed a bit by now.'

I give a little laugh. 'He's a millionaire to begin with.'

'Yeah, right, there's that,' says Crash, but somehow I sense he's not thinking about the money.

Zia

I kept telling myself that it was the music that mattered to me. I was down to do a solo act at the school concert, but ever since I had heard Sam's voice singing my songs, the way she and I worked in harmony, I knew that we just had to perform together.

I had started thinking that maybe she was more interested in Mark and going to a stupid football match than my songs, but as it turned out I needn't have worried. The day after I gave her the tape, she came up to me in the playground and quietly sang in my ear the chorus of 'Private Cloud'.

I smiled. Even sung softly, it sounded better than I had imagined.

'What say we run through them together after school?' she said.

I winced. The fact is, my parents are not too keen on my playing the guitar. 'My house is kind of crowded,' I said.

'Come over to my place,' she said. 'Bring a guitar and a tape and we'll lay down a couple of tracks together.'

'Would that be all right with Mr and Mrs Burton?'

'Sure,' she said. 'They're pussy cats.' And she gave me this enormous smile, looking deep into my eyes as if she knew me better than I know myself.

My stomach lurched. It's the music, I told myself. Just the music.

But in my heart I knew that it wasn't.

Matthew

Weirdly, the fact that his long-lost dad was on his case had seemed to calm Sam down. He no longer had to be the centre of attention all the time. Between lessons he talked to us almost as much as he talked to Elena and her gang, with the result that we all eased up on each other.

An example. One day that week – Tuesday, I think – he was walking home with Tyrone, Jake and me. We had been talking about how Tyrone's mum had been treating him with new respect ever since he had rolled up with an American girlfriend. The only problem was that Mrs Sherman kept saying, 'And how's T-Bone today?' and asking after 'that nice American girl'.

Mrs Sherman

I decided to relax about my son that week. It had turned out that he was making his way in the world without the help of his old mum. Even the problem of his waistline was not a problem, after all. I was terribly relieved and happy for us both.

One last thing needed to be done. Now that Tyrone had decided to be a highly successful businessman when he grew up, it would be a good idea for him to get a head start over other boys and girls.

I started to make enquiries about private tutors specialising in business studies and accounting. It would be my secret project until the moment when I could spring this lovely surprise on my son.

I couldn't wait to see his face.

Matthew

On the other hand, Jake had been kind of moody over the past few days. He had listened to the stories of Tyrone and his girlfriend, of the visit of Mr and Mrs Crash to my house, of how my mum and dad had amazed us by agreeing to let Sam remain a girl, but he had seemed kind of cut off from it all, as if he had other, bigger things on his mind than a guy dressed up as a girl hiding from this hoodlum dad.

Sam must have picked up on his because, as we made our way through the park, he said, 'And how's life in the world of Jakey?'

Maybe Jake heard an echo of the old mockery in Sam's voice because a hooded, defensive look came over his face. 'What's it to you?' he said.

'You seem kind of out of it,' said Sam easily. 'I was just wondering if everything was OK with you?'

'Share with the group, you mean.' Jake gave an unconvincing sneer. 'You've been with those girls too long.'

'Easy, Jake,' said Tyrone. 'He was only asking.'

'All this family talk is doing my head in,' Jake muttered. We were passing the bench where the Shed Gang used to meet. It had been a while since we had spent time there, but now Sam sat down and, smoothing his skirt thoughtfully over his knees, said, 'I ain't too happy playing the family game either.'

Jake kicked a stone against the wall.

'How's your dad these days?' Sam asked.

Jake swore quietly in reply. Then, scuffing the ground with his foot, he started talking about what had been going on back home.

It turned out that with all this talk of dads and mums, we had been doing a little dance all over Jake's corns. Ever since his father had left home, he had been living in this all-girl household with his mother and his sister. Things had not been too great with the Smileys over the past two years as the marriage cracked and crumbled.

Now that he was the only male in the house, it seemed that his mother was permanently irritated by him – by the state of his room, and the way he dressed and spoke and didn't seem to be making any progress at school.

His sixteen-year-old sister had joined the attack, forever complaining about things he had done or not done or done in the wrong way.

'Every day this...chorus of complaint follows me around,' said Jake. 'I just need to walk into a room round at my place and I'm already annoying somebody.'

'You're a guy,' said Sam. 'Your mom's on your case because she's mad at your dad. Your sister is picking up on the vibe.'

'What are you, some kind of shrink?' Jake gave an empty little laugh.

'What does your dad say?' I asked.

'What dad?' said Jake. 'I haven't seen him for a month.

He calls me once a week and that's it.'

There was a moment's silence. Then, as if realising that he had given too much away, Jake stood up. 'I gotta go,' he said.

'You know what you do?' Sam looked up at Jake. 'You call your dad. You tell him you'd like to meet up. You talk it through.'

'I'm not the parent, he is,' said Jake. 'He's the one who left home.'

'Believe me,' said Sam. 'Maybe he feels so bad about what's happened that he's ashamed to show you how he feels. Maybe your mom has said something to him. You've got to talk to him, Jake. Call him or message him and see what happens.'

But Jake was on his way, hands in his pockets, his bony shoulders hunched, closed in on himself and his unhappiness.

Crash

Here's the Crash Lopez three-point method: watch, learn, make your move fast and hard, get the hell out of there. Maybe it was four points.

That week we watched. We took in the sights, cruised the area in that embarrassment of a toy car, generally blended in with the scenery. We tried to get used to the way the natives spoke – the 'pleases', the 'thank yous', the 'are-you-sures'.

I still had this niggling sense that the creepy Burton family was holding out on me, so that Tuesday

197

evening, we hung out on Somerton Gardens, sitting in the car, heads behind newspapers, watching and waiting.

It turned out they had a visitor that night – some little Indian chick, carrying a guitar case, came back with the Burton kid and the Canadian girl, Simone. As night closed in we heard the sound of singing coming from the house.

'It's the girls singing,' said Ottoleen. 'It sounds nice, doesn't it?'

I said it sounded OK through a couple of walls. Maybe close to, it wouldn't be so great.

'Family life,' said Ottoleen in that dreamy voice, which kind of gives me the creeps to tell the truth.

'Don't even think what you're thinking,' I said. 'We're getting my son back first, right?'

'I never said anything about starting our very own family. I never even mentioned how totally great it would be or how happy it would make me.'

I looked across. She was giving me that smile she knows I can't resist.

'Honey,' I said. 'Starting a family is serious. It's not an easy thing, like starting a car or starting a fight.'

'It can be easy,' she said, and squeezed my knee.

The singing from the house stopped for a moment. Then the girls started their song again.

'I can't stand this waiting,' I said. 'I need action.'

'Sure, Crash.' Ottoleen cuddled closer. 'I guess we all need a bit of action sometimes.'

Zia

It was one of the most magical moments of my life.

Sam and I had gone straight to her little room, leaving Matthew downstairs watching TV.

I got my guitar out of the case, tuned it. 'Where shall we start?' I asked.

'How about "Private Cloud"?' she said. 'That's the single, right?'

I laughed, played the intro chords, then stopped. I find I can play in public, but performing for one or two makes me feel shy.

Then Sam started singing, she picked up the key from me and went ahead by herself.

> *'They say – take it easy, take it slow*
> *They say – give it time and let it grow*
> *They tell me take it one day at a time*
>
> *They say – that caution never fails*
> *One day – the wind will catch my sails*
> *And take me through the shadowland, the*
> * second hand*
> *And soon I'm gonna climb.*

The opening verse sounded so good coming from her that my fingers started moving over the frets almost of their own accord. When she reached the chorus, I came in with a harmony. Soon, smiles on our faces, looking into each other's eyes, we're singing together.

'And I'll be high in the sky
Looking down on the world
Me on my private cloud
Living my daydreams
Wherever I go
Singing my life out loud.'

It was all I could do not to cry with the feelings that were welling up inside me. But Sam was already hitting the second verse.

Magical. I'll never forget it.

Matthew

I was downstairs when these voices started coming through the ceiling. At first I thought that Sam and Zia had put on a record.

I turned down the sound on the TV and listened more closely. It was the two of them, singing to the guitar, and it was – well, would 'unbelievable' do?

16

Mrs Cartwright

I was in my office one morning during the second week of term when I received a call from a Mr Stevenson, an American gentleman. He informed me that he was moving into the area and that he had a kid, as he put it, that he would like to enrol at the school. He would very much like to 'check out' the school.

Between you and me, I was not overly impressed by his tone of voice. I informed him that there were certain procedures involved.

'Procedures?' he said. 'What's there to proceed? Me and my wife want to look round your school. How does tomorrow sound?'

I told him that we had what I call proper channels for prospective parents. Our next open day would be in eight days' time. From seven o'clock the following Thursday, he and his wife would be welcome to visit the school and meet myself and some of the other teachers.

I heard him discussing the matter with Mrs Stevenson.

'We normally advise parents to bring the child in question along with them,' I said. 'Is it a boy or a girl?'

'Er, he's a guy,' said Mr Stevenson. 'Name of...' He hesitated. 'Name of Angelo.'

'Angelo is very welcome,' I said.

He muttered something, which sounded like, 'Yeah, yeah,' and hung up.

Slowly I put down the receiver. I remember hoping that Angelo had better manners than his father if he wanted to what I call fit in at Bradbury Hill School.

Matthew

I just didn't get it. As if Sam's life wasn't complicated enough, he was now planning to go out on a date. What was more, he seemed quite excited about it.

'You can cancel, you know,' I said to him as we made our way to school on the morning of his big night out with Mark Kramer.

'Why on earth would I want to do that?' Sam said with a little shake of his long hair.

'Because you've got enough problems.'

'I can handle them.'

'Because cancelling things is what girls do.'

'Not this girl.'

'Because you're a guy, for God's sake!' I almost forgot myself and shouted the words out loud.

He smiled and shook his head. 'Sometimes you are so old-fashioned.'

Charley

I don't care what she said, Sam was excited about her date with Mark Kramer. Everyone in the class had heard that Mark was taking her to a football game. Although some of the girls teased her, it was pretty clear that they were impressed.

After all, it was unusual for a boy in the Lower Sixth to pay any attention to a Year Eight girl. For the boy to be Signor Hunko himself was quite an event.

In the playground, between classes, we noticed that some of the older girls were darting looks at Sam, as if they were thinking to themselves, 'What exactly has this little kid got to offer that we haven't?'

Sam seemed pretty cool about it all, but I could tell that the attention was getting to her. The rest of us, perhaps with one exception, were just proud of her.

Elena

So what was the big deal? He probably wouldn't show or he'd roll up with that Tasha, just as he did with me.

Anyway, the way I saw it, where would Sam have been without my padded bra?

Mr Burton

When Matthew mentioned that he was worried about Sam going to a football match with this older boy, Mary and I had a big discussion about how best to handle the situation.

Obviously, to the outside world there would be a problem. It was clearly inappropriate that a girl of thirteen should be dating a boy four years older than her, particularly if the boy in question has a bit of a reputation.

On the other hand, Sam wasn't a girl. What was happening here was that a couple of boys were going to a football match. Why, if one of the boys happened to be disguised as a girl, should that make any difference?

For some reason, it did. We were concerned. Somehow it seemed all wrong.

Mrs Burton

Neither of us mentioned it, but I knew we were both thinking the same thing. Sam was enjoying being a girl rather too much for this to be entirely straightforward.

He plucked his eyebrows. He had become concerned about what he wore. He had taken to giggling. Frankly, if one night he had volunteered to cook us a nice new vegetarian dish he had been working on and had announced that he wanted to be a hairdresser when he grew up, we would not have been in the least surprised.

Gender fluid. Neither of us actually said the phrase out loud, but at this point it was on our minds.

Not that we had a problem with that. Gender fluid was fine with us, so long as it was what Sam really wanted. But was it?

Mark

Looking back on it, we should have gone to the family stand, or maybe the south enclosure – anywhere, in fact, except the Pit. Because the Pit, where the most hardcore fans hung out, was definitely not a place for girls. But tickets for the Pit were the only ones that weren't sold out. Sam said she wanted excitement and atmosphere.

She got it.

Everyone's different outside school, but Sam Lopez was way, way different that night. The crowd was gathering outside the main entrance when I first caught sight of her and, if it hadn't been for that long blonde hair, I wouldn't have recognised her. She walked through the fans with a kind of bouncy swagger, looking this way and that, wide-eyed and with a dangerous half-smile on her face. She wore jeans and trainers and a big purple puffa jacket that somehow made her look even smaller than usual.

'Whoa,' she said when I greeted her. 'This is more like it.'

'I knew you'd like football,' I said.

'It ain't the football,' she said, looking around her. 'It's the violence. I can smell it in the air.'

'Don't worry,' I said in my most reassuring voice. 'I'll look after you.'

She looked up at me and laughed in a way which I found kind of peculiar. It was almost as if she felt sorry for me.

We took our seats and, by the time the game had started, I knew that I had made a big mistake bringing a girl to the Pit. Looking around me I saw some familiar faces, the hard men and psychos who turn out for the games when the heaviest action is going to be off the pitch.

Sam hardly watched the football, but looked around her as the supporters jeered and cheered and chanted and goaded the other side's fans, who were in the north stand.

Then she started joining in. Within a few minutes, she was screaming abuse with the best of them. Normally I like a bit of a shout myself, but the more noise Sam made beside me, the more I wished we were somewhere else – at a cinema, a restaurant, anywhere but in the Pit during a derby-cup game.

Because soon the fans around us were noticing this crazy little American chick and her wild language.

'Go for it, girl,' one of them shouted after she had stood up alone and directed a few choice swear words in the direction of the other fans.

'Easy, Sam,' I muttered.

She glanced at me and I noticed a dangerous glint in her eye. 'Got a problem, hombre?' she said.

I shrugged and said nothing.

It was five minutes before the end of the game when the real trouble started. The other side scored in the goal just in front of us and, as their players celebrated, a few of the rival fans, not fifty metres from us, ran out to the pitch to join in the party.

It was too much for some of our guys. They were out of their seats and on to the turf before the stewards could do anything about it.

I turned to Sam to suggest that maybe we should leave – just in time to see her leap up, run down the aisle nearby, skip over the low fence and into the small riot that was already developing on the pitch.

It got worse. More fans became involved. The players left the pitch, and about ten police horses, their riders in full riot gear, emerged from the far corner of the ground and advanced in a line towards the fighting fans.

What could I do? Chase Sam on to the pitch? Pull her out of there? It was too late. She was in the thick of it all, legs and fists flying. I decided that I should stay where I was. At least that way she would know where to find me when things calmed down.

But she showed no sign of turning back. One or two of the other side's fans seemed to hesitate when they saw this little girl in the front line of the action. It was a mistake. With a kick to the crotch or a fist to the face, Sam was on them.

With the horses trying to separate the two groups of fans, some of them decided they had had their fun and returned, grinning and punching the air, to their seats. Soon only about fifty or so remained battling it out on the pitch. Sam, as is now well known, was in the thick of it all. I ran to the front row of seats and screamed at her from behind the line of stewards, who were now shoulder to shoulder, preventing anyone else from getting to the pitch.

Too late. The remaining fans were cornered by the horses. Police with dogs moved in and, amid a blizzard of flashing bulbs from the press photographers who had gathered around the scene, they were grabbed, one after another and frogmarched off to the vans outside, to cheers and boos from the fans in the stand.

That was the last I saw of Sam on our great night out – walking between two policemen, each of them twice her size, as photographers snapped away and people in the crowd pointed at her.

No one – not a player, not a fan – had made such an impact as Sam Lopez did that evening.

Mr Burton

At around ten that night, we got a call from Mark Kramer.

'Something's happened,' he said.

He told me the police station that Sam had been taken to. I said I was on my way.

Matthew

You want the truth? Part of me was relieved when the call from Kramer came through and we learned the sad news of how Sam's hot date had ended.

The fact is, it could have been a whole lot worse. Sooner or later Mark would have tried it on or said or done something that would have offered Sam a choice – either smack him in the chops or reveal his guilty secret.

The fact that he had got involved in a football riot and had ended up in the police cells solved that problem at least.

Sam – the real Sam – was back. That night he had put away his eyebrow tweezers, had gone out and, as he once would have put it, had kicked some serious ass, just like in the old days back in the States.

It had turned out that you can dress someone up in a skirt, get him to mix with female company, give him all the things a girl might want, but when it came right down to it, a guy was a guy.

I can't say that the idea upset me too much.

PC Chivers

It was a rough night. We took the home fans in, put them in the cells, charged some of the worst troublemakers, and let the rest off with a caution after allowing them to cool down for a few hours.

Some of the lads were worried about leaving a young girl with some of the hard cases we had arrested, but we didn't have a choice. Besides, the two officers who had brought her in seemed to think that she was capable of looking after herself.

Soon after eleven, a Mr Burton appeared, asking for her. We took him into the interview room, and brought the girl Lopez in and told them both that, in view of her age and the fact that she had probably been led astray by some of the undesirable older male elements she had been mixing with, she was going to be released with a formal caution.

Mr Burton seemed relieved, but the girl just sat glowering at us, as if all this was somehow our fault.

We were about to let them go, when the duty officer suggested that, since Mr Burton was not her father, we should check that he was genuinely the girl's guardian.

I put through the call to the number Mr Burton gave. Mrs Burton explained the situation but seemed less than impressed by what had occurred. So Miss Lopez was released from custody, and frankly I would have liked to be a fly on the wall when that little girl got home.

Funnily enough, it was only later that I realised why there had been something familiar about her. I had seen her before – in the park, hanging about with some boys.

Honestly, kids these days. It makes you wonder sometimes.

Mrs Burton

They were home after midnight. It took one look at Sam for me to realise that now was not the moment for us to talk this thing through.

His jeans were torn and the purple puffa jacket that he had been so proud of was covered with dust and mud. There was a red welt across his cheek and the beginnings of what looked like a nasty black eye.

He ignored me as he walked into the kitchen.

'I'm starved,' he muttered as he opened the bread bin, took out a couple of slices and rammed them down into the toaster.

'Are you all right?' Matthew asked.

'Sure? Why not?' said Sam.

'We'll talk about this tomorrow.' I spoke quietly, darting a warning look at David and Matthew.

'Talk about what?' he said.

The toast jumped up. Sam grabbed a piece and started buttering it without bothering to use a plate. He took a large mouthful.

'So,' he said aggressively, taking us all in with a withering glance. 'That was soccer, eh?' He chewed for a moment. 'Tell you what – I like it.'

17

Mrs Cartwright

It was not a good day. Within moments of my arrival at the office, Mrs Burton had rung to tell me that Sam Lopez had been in what she described as 'a spot of trouble'.

The spot of trouble turned out to be participating in a full-scale riot at a local football match. I was concerned to learn that Sam had been at the game in the company of Mark Kramer, one of the less reliable boys in the Lower Sixth.

I explained to Mrs Burton that, while it was important to stress that Bradbury Hill had no responsibility for what pupils did in their spare time, I would speak both to her and the boy, Kramer.

I put down the phone. Frankly this was all I needed. We have always come down very hard on any form of hooliganism at this school and I had thought that it was a problem that we had under control. It seemed I was wrong – even Year Eight girls were likely to go off the tracks and start behaving like boys.

I thought back to the day last week when I had caught a group of girls playing American football in the playground. The look that Sam Lopez had given me that day, cold and insolent, had set off alarm bells and, as is depressingly usual, my instinct was right. That young girl had always been particularly vulnerable – no wonder that the older boys were able to pass on what I call their less-than-desirable habits to her.

There was a knock on the door. It was Karen O'Grady, my secretary. She was carrying a newspaper.

'Sorry to bother you, head teacher,' she said. 'But I think you should see this.'

She laid the newspaper before me. Beneath a one-word headline, 'HELLCAT', a photograph filled most of the page. It showed a scene of utter confusion – policemen, football fans, fists and feet. There, in the very centre of the action, lunging out with her foot, her face concealed by swirling blonde hair, was a small doll-like figure who would have seemed completely out of context were it not for the fact that her foot was about to make contact with a figure crouched on the ground.

'Journalists have started calling,' Karen said. 'They aren't allowed to name her, but someone from the police must have tipped them off that she goes to Bradbury Hill.'

I felt a lurch of dread from within. The years of work that I had put in at this school were in jeopardy. My whole career, my reputation as what I call an educational high-flyer, would be shattered by this kind of publicity.

'Tell them I have no comment to make,' I said. 'Remind them that the school has no responsibility for what its pupils do in their spare time.'

'Yes, head teacher.'

'And, I'll need to see Mark Kramer and Sam Lopez after assembly.'

'Yes, head teacher.'

'And, give me five minutes, will you?'

Karen nodded. 'Cupboard, head teacher?'

'Yes,' I said. 'Cupboard.'

Elena

I couldn't believe it. When Charley and I arrived at school that morning, the word was out about Sam and Mark getting caught up in the football riot. There were little knots of people in the playground, each gathered around a copy of a newspaper with Sam's 'HELLCAT' shot on the front.

'She's here,' someone said.

We turned to see Sam making her way through the school gates with Matthew. Even from a distance, I could see that one of Sam's eyes was black and swollen. They walked slowly, and as Sam became aware that heads were turning towards her, a hard little smile appeared on her lips. One of the Year Seven girls called out, 'Way to go, Sam.' She lifted a hand like she was some kind of all-conquering hero acknowledging her fans.

If there's one thing that I don't like it's a show-off. 'She's lapping it up,' I said to Charley. 'Anyone would think it was clever, taking part in a riot and appearing in the papers.'

Sam had stopped to talk to Jake and Tyrone. She exercised a sort of kicking movement, as if showing them exactly how it had all happened, then laughed in a showy kind of way.

'So how do we stand on this?' Charley asked. 'Is she a friend or an ex-friend?'

'She's a hooligan, that's for sure,' I said.

'Exactly,' said Charley. 'I don't approve of violence.'

'Nor me.'

Sam was walking towards us, the way clearing before her and, seeing that look of triumph on her face, complete with a black eye that a panda would have been proud of, I just had to smile. Charley turned to me and gave a kind of resigned shrug.

'Hi, Sam,' we said in unison.

Matthew

Sam loved it. He made another of his entrances. The guy was a natural exhibitionist and this was his big moment – yet another big moment.

And the people at school – older, younger, boys, girls – actually thought it was cool what he had done. When it became known that a picture of Sam Lopez brutalising some football fan had appeared on the front page of a newspaper, he became this big star. 'Hey, Hellcat!' people would call out as Sam swaggered by, skirt swishing proudly.

I was thinking to myself, Hang on, we're talking about someone kicking and punching a stranger here. Is that really a good reason to turn them into a celebrity?

But no. Sam had been touched by fame. It didn't

matter how he'd done it. The fame was what mattered.

And when Mrs O'Grady marched up and told him that the head wanted to see him right now, he seemed even more pleased with himself.

Mrs Cartwright

It's a wonderful release, the cupboard. Other head teachers use therapists or perhaps even take a tranquillising pill now and then, but I prefer to what I call let it all out by having a good scream in the privacy of my cupboard.

My secretary, Karen, a marvellous woman who has been with me ten years now, understands the importance of having these moments of privacy, and I do not for a moment blame her for what happened on this occasion.

I was in the cupboard, eyes closed in the cool, welcome darkness. I went through my usual routine. For a moment or two, I allowed my brain to fill with what I call stress sources. I gathered them together as if they were little more than a pile of dust that could be blown away, one by one, by the sheer force of screaming. I took a deep breath.

I thought of...football hooligans.

'Aarrgghh!'

I paused, panting slightly. Then I thought of...gutter journalists.

'Aaaarrrrgggghhh!'

I was feeling better now. One more scream and I would be healed, cleansed.

I thought of...Sam Lopez.

'AAAARRRGGGHHHH!'

It was an excellent scream – long, loud, healthy, one of my very best. When I had finished, I felt a new person. I was in control, a head teacher once more. I shook my head briskly, squared my shoulders, opened the cupboard door – and found myself staring into the face of Sam Lopez.

'Feeling better, Mrs Cartwright?' she said, lolling in my guest chair, a big smile on her impertinent little face.

'I was, um, looking for some stationery,' I said.

'Sure you were,' she said. 'It's good to get things off your chest now and then, isn't it?'

I sat down behind my desk and held up the day's newspaper. 'Would you care to explain this?'

She shrugged and touched her right eye, which was dark and swollen. 'I guess I was letting off a bit of steam too.'

I took a deep breath and began to give her a lecture about responsibility, but I was not exactly at my best after what had just happened. After a minute or so, I told Lopez to fetch the boy, Kramer.

'You don't want to worry about old Marky.' She stood up. 'He's clean.'

I told her that I would be the one to decide who was 'clean' or not.

'Sure you will,' said Lopez. She winked at me with her good eye. 'Sure you will.'

Zia

I was a bit late that morning. By the time I arrived everyone was talking about Sam and Mark Kramer and the big bust-up at the game.

I didn't talk to her, but I could see she was happy. It was as if she were a princess who had assumed her kingdom, a bad girl come good.

Throughout the day, I had only one thought.

Bad girl. A bad girl come good. Bad girl, bad girl, with the baddest kind of fame. It was going to be a terrific song.

Ottoleen

By now Crash is getting kind of antsy about waiting around. It's getting to him that we're spending money on the hotel and the Nissan with no sign of a return on our investment. Now and then he talks about making some kind of small hit and earning himself some more – with Crash, earning means taking and it's never a problem – but in the end we decide to lie low until we can get to the school.

It's fair to say that England is not exactly impressing old Crash. One day that week, as we're eating one of the hotel's totally barfsome breakfasts, he shows me the page of a paper he is reading.

It's some kind of yak-yak piece headlined 'NOW EVEN OUR LITTLE GIRLS ARE YOBS', but it's the picture underneath that is bothering him. It was a little blonde kid, kicking the you-know-what out of an older boy during some kind of sports bust-up. She must be twelve – thirteen, tops.

'That's a child, for pity's sake. A girl too.' He shakes his head. 'What a country.' Then he looks a bit closer at the paper. He goes, 'Where have I seen that face before?'

Crash

I'd seen enough to know that it was time to make our move. This was no place for a son of mine to be raised in. I rang the principal that morning.

We needed to see the school pronto, I said. We were going away for a while. It was kind of urgent.

She sounded distracted, like she had other things on her mind.

'Maybe Talent Night would be a good opportunity,' she said. All the children and teachers would be there, and some of the parents.

Talent night? I was thinking. What would I want to go to a kids' talent night for? But then, maybe, with all sorts of stuff going down, it occurred to me that we could check out the place and find my boy.

'Sure,' I said. 'That would be really nice.'

I hung up the phone and frowned.

Really nice? Did I just say that? We had to get out of here before it was too late.

Steve Forrester

I had a decision to make that week. The new girl, Sam, had become involved in unpleasant scenes at a football game, albeit I suspected that an older boy, Mark Kramer, was primarily responsible for what had happened – Sam, for all her bravado, was essentially a very impressionable young girl – but clearly violence is violence, whatever the circumstances.

I decided to make no reference in class to what had happened that evening, but to make it quite clear from my attitude towards Sam that I disapproved of her behaviour.

I think that taught her a useful lesson about the way we do things in this country. She settled down and spent more and more time with Zia Khan. Together they seemed to be involved in some kind of musical project.

Zia

It turned out that my timing was perfect. When I gave Sam the lyrics and melody for 'Bad Girl' she was in precisely the right mood to give it the kind of edgy vocals that I was looking for.

The day after I had written it, we practised back at the Burton house. Even before she had completely mastered the tune, she was giving the song a kind of brooding menace that made the hairs on the back of my neck prickle.

There was a small problem. The chorus, which went

into a short Latino hip-hop riff, needed more voices, singing – or rather shouting – across the lead vocal. I could do it myself, but we needed a crowd, gang-like, girls-against-the-world feel. I'd need to think about that.

Sam had been hard-eyed and surly since her date with Mark Kramer, but, as we sang together in her bedroom, she seemed to loosen up. In fact, she even came up with a dramatic musical idea herself.

She was singing the final verse, driving the vocals hard, when something odd happened. When she went for the high note on the last line, her voice, instead of going up the scale, suddenly went down into a sort of dog-like growl.

I stopped playing. 'What was that?' I asked.

Sam looked embarrassed. She cleared her throat. 'Nothing.'

'Is the key too high for you? I could modulate there if you like?'

'Nah.' Sam cleared her throat again. 'I just figured that maybe we could use a howl at that point in the song.'

'A howl?'

'Yeah. Like the Warren Zevon thing in "Werewolves of London", you know the Warren Zevon thing?' she said.

I shook my head. Sam was always coming up with bands and songs from ancient history that I had never heard of.

'Yeah, the Zevon howl would be good,' she said. 'We've got to get the howl in.'

We tried it again, changing one of the chords, going slow so that she could hit the right note, only this time I went up with her, following her with a descant harmony, but dragging it so that there was a kind of weird and scary dissonance to it.

The third time, we really went for it. The door burst open and Matthew stood there, hands over his ears.

'Are you guys torturing cats in here?' he said. 'That sounds terrible.'

Sam looked at me and gave me the big smile that I liked so much.

'I think we're in business,' she said.

Elena

It was on Thursday when Zed and Sam came ambling up to Charley and me during breaktime. I could tell that from the grins they were trying to keep off their faces that they had something on their minds.

'Here's the thing,' said Sam. 'Our little resident musical genius here has come up with a killer song that we're going to play at the concert.'

'I thought Zia was doing a solo act,' I said suspiciously.

'Not any more,' said Zia. 'Sam and I are doing a song called "Private Cloud". Then we were thinking of doing a band number.'

'Band?' said Charley. 'And who exactly is the band?'

Charley

Forget it. This was the craziest idea I had ever heard. First of all, we had a day – two, max – in which to rehearse it.

Second, Elena's got a voice like someone scraping their nails down a blackboard.

Elena

Luckily I've got quite a good voice (though I say so myself) and a really excellent stage presence. I was a bit worried about Charley – she's not exactly showbiz material – but the way I saw it, the rest of us could cover for her.

Charley

That night, back at my place, Zia played us a tape of the song. It was kind of strange, but catchy too.

'So what do we do?' I asked.

'You shout that chorus line, just as loud as you can,' said Zia.

'Shout?' said Elena. 'I thought you wanted us to sing.'

And Zia went into this routine about how the timing was really subtle, and how the shouting bit was the most important part of the whole song.

'How about if I sang the second verse?' said Elena.

There was a moment's pause and, for an instant, it seemed as if someone was going to have to tell her that Elena Griffiths singing anything solo would clear the school hall in ten seconds flat. To my amazement, it was Sam who saved the day.

'There are a lot of lyrics to learn,' she said. 'And we were really hoping you could do a kind of funky dance – like, add a bit of sexy glamour to the whole thing.'

Elena gave the matter serious thought for a couple of seconds. 'Sexy glamour? Yeah, maybe I could do that.'

Jake

There are some things you can't talk to people about. Matt and Tyrone knew that I was having a tough time at home – I could see it in their eyes, hear it in their voices. These days when they said, 'All right, then?' it was more than just a greeting. But talking about that sort of stuff is just plain embarrassing.

All the same, my problems were weighing on my shoulders like a bag of cement. In the past, when I still had a real family, I could have opened up to my mum, or even my sister Chrissie, but now it was different.

Within seconds, the discussion would have become an argument which would have developed into a row with all the same old stuff spilling out like dirty laundry. How I didn't help. How I never talked. How I was a lump. How I was useless.

'Typical man,' Mum would say.

'That is such a male attitude,' Chrissie would join in.

And there would be laughter, hard and brittle, although each of us knew in our hearts that none of this was even slightly funny.

That Friday lunchtime, I was enjoying a bit of quality time on my own in the yard when Sam Lopez, hellcat and school hero, noticed me and wandered over.

Casually, he started chatting about this and that – about things that were going on in his life, how he was going to appear at the school concert with Zia Khan, and so on. I responded with polite grunts. To tell the truth, the life and times of little boy2girl Sam were beginning to get on my nerves.

'How's that old man of yours?' The question came out of nowhere.

'He's fine,' I said automatically.

'Meaning you ain't talked to him, right?'

'Meaning he hasn't called me. My father's a pretty busy man.'

Sam looked at me, all cool and narrow-eyed. 'It's like I told you. Sometimes you have to make the first move.'

'Thanks for the advice, Mr Family Expert.'

A couple of weeks ago, Sam might have lost it at this point, but now he just smiled. 'You coming to the concert tomorrow night?'

I shrugged. 'I didn't want to, but my mum insisted. It's the kind of thing she likes to be seen at. It makes her feel like a real parent.'

'Lose her.'

'What?'

'Lose your mum. There'll be other concerts for her to go to. Tell your dad you'd like him to be there.'

'It's a Saturday night. He'll have things planned.'

'I'll bet you ten quid he accepts.'

'I'm not sure, Sam.'

'Sometimes you have to be more adult than the adults.'

It was at that moment I noticed Mark Kramer walking towards us, followed by a couple of his friends from the Lower Sixth, Dan Collins and Liam Murphy.

Mark

I'd had it up to here with the comments. For two days, guys in my class had been giving me grief about my date with Sam. They said that they had heard I'd been hiding in the stands while she was out there, mixing it with the away fans. I'd been shown up by a little Year Eight girl. I wasn't the cool, hard guy that I like to make out. They said that maybe I should try one of the Year Seven girls next time. It was getting beyond a joke.

Between you and me, I wasn't exactly crazy about going out with Sam again. The way she had been that night had broken the spell. Maybe deep down I'm old-fashioned about this but, given the choice (and Mark Kramer does have the choice, believe me), I'd prefer to go out with a girl who behaves more or less like a girl.

On the other hand, there was a principle involved. Mark Kramer does not allow some skinny little kid to make him look stupid in front of his friends.

So here was what I was going to do. I was going to take her out this weekend. We'd go somewhere safe where there was no danger of her getting into a fight. I'd make her my girlfriend, like it or not. Then I'd dump her.

Back at school, the word would soon be out. Mark had hooked up with Sam. The natural order had returned. Mr Heartbreak was back in town.

Matthew

You know how, when they're showing those wildlife documentaries, herd animals act together almost as if they are part of one huge body. That's the way it is at school. Nobody has to say that there's trouble about. It's in the air. Almost before it happens, the whole herd is on red alert.

I was talking to Tyrone when I noticed Mark and a couple of other boys moving in on Sam and Jake. There was something in the way Mark stood between his two mates, as if he were squaring up to Sam, that suggested that they were not just shooting the breeze.

We decided to take a closer look.

Zia

I was with Charley and Elena and we were looking for Sam to fix up a band rehearsal that night. She was nowhere to be seen.

Then we saw her in the corner of the playground. She was surrounded by boys.

Mark

No way was I threatening her. All I wanted was for a couple of the guys to be there to see with their own eyes that Mark Kramer hadn't lost his touch. And, if they were on each side of me as I talked to Sam, so what? How were they meant to stand – in single file?

'Hey, cupcake,' I said, nice and friendly.

She glanced away briefly from her little friend, whatever his name was. 'Fade,' she said.

'That eye of yours all right, is it?'

'Sure. No problems.' She turned back to her friend.

'What you doing Saturday night, babe?' Sam seemed not to hear me. 'Wanna take in a club?' I said.

'I'm busy,' she said. 'Oh, and by the way, just for the record, I'm not your babe.'

I laughed and winked at a couple of Year Eight kids, Matthew and Tyrone, who had wandered over and were listening in. 'That's not what she said the other day,' I told them.

This remark seemed to take a while to sink into Sam's pretty little head. Then she took a step towards me.

'Why don't you just go sit on it?' she said quietly. 'I'm singing at the concert tomorrow night and, even if I wasn't, I'd rather die than be seen out with a loser like you.'

'Oh yeah?' I groped in my mind for a killer comeback line but, unusually, there was nothing there. 'Why's that then?'

Elena

Sam just smiled slowly, her eyes fixed on Mark's. 'Why am I not going out with you?' she said. 'Because I'm going out with someone else.'

Charley and I looked at each other, eyes wide. This was news – big news.

'Yeah, right.' Mark chuckled nastily. 'And who exactly would that be, little girl?'

Sam shrugged, and walked slowly towards the least likely candidate for boyfriendhood in the whole of Bradbury Hill.

Tyrone

Whaaat?

Matthew

Tyrone tried to smile. When Sam slung an arm over his big shoulders, he made as if to pull away, but Sam held on tight.

'I don't believe it,' said Charley. 'Tyrone? He's so... I mean, he's so Tyrone.'

'She's kidding,' said Mark. 'Who'd want to go out with a little fat kid?'

'You're jealous,' said Sam. 'Ty's twice the man you are.' Suddenly all eyes were on Tyrone, the surprise stud of Bradbury Hill.

He swallowed hard. 'I think you've bothered my girlfriend enough,' he said, his voice shaking slightly.

Mark ignored him and stared at Sam. 'You are so dead, little girl,' he said. He turned away and walked off with as much dignity as he could manage, followed by Dan and Liam.

'Congratulations,' I said Jake, shaking his head in wonderment. 'True love strikes again.'

'I'm shocked,' said Charley.

'Never trust the quiet ones,' I said.

'I don't believe it.' It was a whisper that came from Zia. 'I just don't believe it.'

Mrs Cartwright

Talent Night at Bradbury Hill, is a marvellous occasion. It gives the kids an opportunity to show off their talents. The parents and future parents can get a sense of what the school is all about and I always make sure that I invite a few influential local councillors and journalists along. It's what I call a harvest festival of publicity for the school.

That said, I felt the merest smidgen of alarm about this year's event.

It had been something of an irregular term. There had been a fight in the playground on the first day, the Year Eight girls had started behaving like boys, two pupils had become involved in a football riot and my spies in the Lower Sixth were suggesting that Mark Kramer was up to some sort of mischief.

It's not in my nature to point the finger of blame at any one individual, but I couldn't help noticing that a common thread ran through all these problems.

That blinking little American girl. What on earth had possessed me to accept her as a pupil?

Tyrone

Big joke. Hilarious. Thanks a bunch, Sam. First he gives my mum the impression that I'm some sort of teenage love god whose secret ambition is to become an accountant. Then he makes sure that I'm public enemy number one for Mark Kramer and his gang by telling the world I'm his major squeeze.

Could it get worse? Of course it could.

'How's that nice girlfriend of yours?' my mother asked me on Friday evening. 'You don't seem to be seeing so much of her these days.'

I shrugged. 'You know what they say – treat 'em mean, keep 'em keen.'

Wrong move.

'Now listen here, Tyrone Sherman.' My mother moved swiftly into responsible-parent mode. 'Just because you happen to be powerfully attractive to the opposite sex, it does not mean that you should treat them badly. I refuse to stand by and see you behaving like some sort of...love rat.'

'I am not a love rat, Mum,' I said wearily. 'The fact is, Sam's been rehearsing a lot for Talent Night tomorrow. She's in a girl band.'

Uh-oh. I caught sight of my mother's expression. I had goofed again.

'Talent night?' she said. 'Tomorrow? I had almost forgotten.'

'Mum, we don't have to—'

'Don't say another word, Tyrone Sherman. You are going to support your girlfriend and that's the end to it.

I can't wait to hear her sing.'

Oh, terrific. That was all I needed.

Charley

It was weird. Ever since Sam had stunned us by revealing that she fancied Tyrone, Zia had gone into a serious decline.

'Forget the rehearsal!' she snapped as we collected our coats at the end of the day. 'The band's history. I'm performing solo.'

'But we're good,' I said. 'What's the problem?'

Zia shook her head. 'You wouldn't understand,' she said.

'But we put in all that work,' said Elena. 'I was going to wear my new crop top.'

'I'm sorry,' said Zia. 'I just can't do it – I can't explain why.'

It was at that moment that Sam appeared.

'I've been looking for you,' she said to Zia. 'We need to talk.'

'Why don't you talk to your darling Tyrone?' said Zia.

'Because I want to talk to you.'

'Forget it,' said Zia.

'I'll walk you home. I've got some news to tell you.'

For the first time I sensed that something odd was going on here and decided to act Miss Kind-and-Tactful. 'We'll call you later,' I said.

Sam and Zia walked away, Sam talking seriously and Zia nodding as she went. They were almost like, I don't know, a couple.

'I don't get it,' said Elena. 'What is that girl's problem?'

'Search me,' I said.

The call from Zia came through within minutes of my getting home.

'About that practice,' she said. 'It's tomorrow at ten – round at Sam's place.'

'I thought the band was breaking up?'

'Not any more.'

'So what changed?'

Zia laughed at the other end of the phone. 'Life, love, showbiz – everything's changed,' she said.

And I had always thought of her as one the sane ones.

Ottoleen

Something about the Brit food seems to disagree with me – suddenly it's Bail City every morning for days. The weather's turned grey and, between you and me, Crash is just not the same as he used to be.

He hasn't hit anyone for a week. He has started drinking English beer. Once, when someone pulled out in front of his Nissan, causing him to brake hard, he just shook his head and laughed. 'These Limeys,' he said, almost affectionately.

That's not right. That's not normal. That's not the Crash Lopez I married.

So, on the day before the school concert, he's suddenly coming on like he really does want to impress the teachers that he is a serious would-be parent. He's bought these terrible clothes – like, a dark-blue blazer and trousers with turn-ups.

'Crash, you look like a crusty old British colonel,' I say, as that Friday evening back in the hotel room he showed me how he was going to look.

'I'm merging, kid,' he says. 'The English don't do fashion – they're famous for it. Snappy dressers make them nervous.'

'Does that mean you won't even be wearing your shades?'

Crash gazes at himself in the mirror. He takes off his shades experimentally, blinks a couple of times, then quickly puts them back on.

'The shades stay,' he goes. 'I can't see without 'em.'

I put my arm around him. 'Then can we go back to the States?' I whisper. 'I'm getting homesick.'

'Sure,' says Crash. 'This time tomorrow we'll be on our way there. Just the three of us. And a nice, fat bank account.'

'Oh great,' I murmur.

But to tell the truth I'm not feeling great about anything right now – least of all there soon being three of us. You know what they say about three being a crowd?

Zia

She told me. He told me. The truth came out as he walked me home that evening. I should have been angry but I wasn't. I was happy, happier than I've ever been in my entire life.

234

She was a he. We were us. And me? I was just living the words of my song.

High in the sky.

Looking down on the world.

Me on my private cloud.

18

Jake

I delayed making the call to my father for as long as possible – sometimes, I thought, if you leave a problem for long enough, it self-corrects – but, by Saturday morning, I had reached that now-or-never moment. I took the cordless phone to my room and dialled the number.

'Jake.' My father sounded surprised and, it seemed to me, rather less than delighted to be hearing from his son. He started asking the usual boring questions about school – anything to avoid talking about what was really going on in his life and mine. I interrupted him.

'There's the school concert tonight. Can you come?'

'Concert? But—' He gave a little laugh. 'You don't play anything.'

That's Dad all right – always the supportive one. 'A friend of mine's playing,' I said. 'I thought you'd like to check up on me with the teachers.'

'Would I ever do that?' he said, playing for time. 'What about your mother?'

'I'm asking you. Please, Dad.'

Silence from the other end of the phone. I was about

to tell him to forget it, when he said, 'I'd really like to, Jake, but I don't want any more trouble with Mum.'

'And if she agrees?'

'I'd love to.'

When I went downstairs, my mother and Chrissie were in the kitchen.

'Mum,' I said. 'Would you mind if I went to the school concert tonight with Dad?'

They both looked at me as if I had said something unspeakably shocking.

'I'm going to the concert, Jake,' said my mother. 'It was agreed.'

'Dad wants to go.'

My mother laughed. 'It's only because he knows it will upset me. That man is so transparent.'

'Yeah,' Chrissie chimed in. 'Like he's been really interested in school concerts before, hasn't he?'

'It was me who asked him,' I said.

'That's nice,' my mother murmured bitterly.

'Mum was really looking forward to that as well,' said Chrissie. 'Honestly, men are just so selfish. It's just me-me-me with them.'

My mother was looking at me, and I knew what the next step would be in this little game. She'd play the guilt card.

'No, that's fine.' She smiled bravely. 'I'll find something to do, I'm sure. I look after you all week, and your father gets the treats at the weekend. That seems pretty much the way it goes these days.'

'It's just that I haven't seen him for a long time.'

'Aaaah,' said Chrissie. 'Let's all feel sorry for Jakey.'

Mum ignored her. Then to my surprise, she nodded. 'For you,' she said. 'Not for him, mind – for you.'

'Thanks, Mum,' I said, and kissed her quickly on the cheek before she had time to move away.

Matthew

I knew that something was up when Sam suggested that I sat in on the rehearsal. Why should the girls want me there? It had to be a non-musical thing.

My parents like to do a big shop on Saturday mornings, which meant that we had the house to ourselves.

The girls arrived together, Zia toting her guitar and grinning as if she had just been told the greatest news ever.

I fetched them drinks from the fridge, as if we were all best friends. Then, as they wandered through to the sitting room, Sam casually mentioned that I was staying for the rehearsal.

'I don't think so,' said Elena, glancing at Zia.

But Zia shrugged as she sat down on the sofa and opened her guitar case. 'I have no problem with that,' she said. 'Maybe it would be useful to have an audience.'

'Zed.' Elena stood, hands on hips, looking profoundly shocked. 'And maybe this should be a band decision.'

Zia glanced at Sam and smiled.

Sam smiled back. It was somehow an unmistakably guy-like smile. Suddenly I knew what was on the way.

He stood up. 'Girls,' he said.

There was something in his tone of voice that caused

Charley and Elena to glance at one another in alarm.

'What do you mean "girls"?' said Charley.

'Are you talking to us?' asked Elena.

Sam spread his arms, enjoying the moment. 'I got something to tell ya.'

Charley

No. Forget it. Impossible. This was some kind of weird Yank wind-up.

But as Sam spoke, I looked first at Zia, then at Matt. 'Is this true?' I asked.

Matt nodded. 'Sam's a boy,' he said. 'Always has been, always will be. It was one of those jokes that got out of hand.'

'*Out of hand?*' This was a sort of shriek from Elena. 'I'll say it got out of hand. You've made fools of us, you dork. We thought you were one of us.'

'I am one of you. El, listen—'

But Elena was on a roll now. 'Think of everything I've done for you. The secrets I've told you, the time I've spent with you, the make-up tips we shared. I even lent you my bra.'

Sam looked down at his chest. 'I'll kind of miss my gazungas,' he said.

'I gave you my tampons,' said Elena in a weak, despairing voice. 'Have you any idea how personal that is? A girl just doesn't share out tampons with anyone.'

'Especially if he's a guy,' murmured Zia unhelpfully.

'I feel so...used,' sniffed Elena.

'I was really grateful,' said Sam. 'At least my problem with Mark was sorted, it being my time of the month and all.'

'Yeah, what about the Mark Kramer thing?' I asked, trying to get the subject away from Elena and her tampons. 'What was all that about?'

Sam shrugged, smiling. 'Between you and me, it was going nowhere, that relationship.'

'He's going to go mad when he finds out,' said Matt, and for a moment the thought of Mr Heartbreak's face when he discovered that his latest girlfriend was a boy eased the tension in the room.

'And now what's going to happen?' I asked.

'Now we play the gig tonight,' said Sam. 'We work out what to do after that.'

Zia was strumming away at her guitar.

'I thought we were a real girl band,' Elena grumbled. 'I'm not sure I'm prepared to do backing vocals for a boy.'

'Pretend I'm a girl one more time,' said Sam. 'Do it for me.'

'And for me,' said Zia, with a little smile.

'Please, El,' said Sam.

Elena

It was the same old story. Yet again the whole future of our band rested on the shoulders of Elena Griffiths. Why is it, I wonder, that it always has to be me who makes the really big decisions?

They were begging me. Basically, I suppose they all realised that, without me, there would be no band – that in a way I was the most important part of the whole line-up.

'I'm really not sure,' I said.

I looked at their anxious faces and made up my mind. Just this once, I'd put my own feelings aside and do it for them.

'All right.' I nodded briskly. 'Let's go.'

And Zia hit the opening chords of 'Bad Girl'.

Matthew

Guitar, then Sam singing solo, Zia coming in on harmonies, building to the chorus with the other two – it was a slow build, 'Bad Girl'.

How did it sound? Not that great, to tell the truth. The four band members seemed to be going in different directions and in different rhythms. Elena and Charley stared at the ground, looking embarrassed. Their shouting bits sounded like kids messing about in a playground. Zia belted her guitar, drawing out the vocals. Even Sam looked as if he wished he were somewhere else.

'Good,' I lied when they had finished.

'You reckon?' said Zia, seeing through my politeness.

'It was…fine.' Anxious to change the subject before the truth came out, I asked, 'What are you guys calling yourselves, by the way?'

Blank looks all round.

Would you believe it? They had formed a band and they didn't even have a name for it.

Tyrone

It only occurred to me that Saturday afternoon when my mother returned from one of her clothes-buying binges that I had a small, Sam-shaped problem on my hands.

I was reading a book on my bed when she waltzed in, looking unusually pleased with herself. She twirled around once and looked at me expectantly.

'Well?' she said.

'Well, what?'

'Well, what do you think of my Talent Night gear? Don't tell me you didn't notice.'

'That thing you're wearing. It's new, isn't it?'

'Honestly, men. They never notice anything. I bet Sam will notice when she sees me tonight.'

I sat up on the bed. Mum, I now realised, had bought herself a new outfit. It was a sort of weird, baggy shirt-and-skirt thing that seemed to be made out of old sacking.

'She's quite a down-to-earth girl, Sam.' My mother did another turn. 'So I wanted a suit that said to her "Ty's mother is an elegant, successful woman, but is also very grounded and sensible and kind". D'you think it says that, Ty?'

'Sam will be up on stage, Mum. She'll have other things on her mind.'

'But afterwards, when the three of us are together in front of all the other parents – me, my son and his lovely, successful girlfriend. And everyone's looking at us. It's important that I look the part.'

'Oh yeah, right. I had forgotten about the other parents.'

'They'll be so jealous of me.' Mum laughed, then suddenly frowned. 'Sam won't think I'm trying to steal her thunder with my new outfit, will she? Teenage girls can be so sensitive about that kind of thing.'

I went back to my book. Mum, I realised, was in for a shock. Just when, for the first time of her life, she thought she could be proud of me, she was going to be more humiliated than ever.

'I'm sure she'll just love it,' I said.

Matthew

Talent Night is kind of a big deal. Mrs Cartwright likes to pretend that the idea is to give the kids a platform to be themselves, to express their music and acting talent, to blahdy-blahdy-blah, but the truth is that it's all about the adults.

Parents are given the chance to see how wonderfully their little ones are getting on. Teachers are able to go around pretending that they're basically normal, straight-forward people. Above all, future parents and a few of the big swells on the local council are shown what a great place Bradbury Hill School has become under the inspired leadership of Mrs Deirdre Cartwright.

It's showbiz, in fact. Nothing but showbiz.

So, unless you're an egomaniac or a teacher's darling, the word on Talent Night is simple: don't.

Last year, I was one of the new kids. Mum and Dad were keen to show what great, committed parents they were. It was bad enough having to watch some acts on the stage but worse – much worse – was seeing teachers trying to be nice. I swore that next year I'd go down with a bad attack of flu rather than repeat the Talent Night experience.

Yet here I was, back again a year later, all because of my little American cousin.

The first people we saw as we arrived at the school that evening were Jake and his father, Mr Smiley. Normally I'd expect Jake to be doing his skulking-in-the-background-wishing-he-was-anywhere-else routine, but when he saw us outside the school gates, he actually stepped forward.

'Hi, Mr and Mrs Burton,' he said, like the nicest kid-next-door you could ever imagine. 'Hi, Matthew. Hi, Sam.'

And Sam does this strange little chuckle. 'Well, hello there, Jakey boy,' he says.

'This is my dad, Sam.' Jake nodded sideways at his father. Now Jake's dad is the ultimate executive-manager type, but that night he was not wearing a suit – in fact, he was not even wearing a tie.

'Hello, young lady,' he said, shaking Sam's hand. 'I've heard all about you.'

'I wouldn't be too sure about that, Mr Smiley,' said Sam. At that moment, he seemed to have noticed something across the room. 'I'd better get ready,' he said and was gone.

Seconds later, Mrs Sherman appeared, wearing a mad, billowing dress and a couple of tons' worth of flashy jewellery. Tyrone was behind her, a wince of embarrassment fixed on his face.

As they joined the group, Mrs Sherman put an arm around Tyrone's broad shoulders. 'Why don't you run after Sam and wish her luck?' she said, loudly enough for us all to hear.

Tyrone muttered something about stage fright.

'Believe me, she'd appreciate it.' Mrs Sherman glanced up at us. 'I know what girls are like. How about a little good-luck kiss?'

My parents must have looked a bit startled by the idea of Tyrone giving Sam a good-luck kiss, because Mrs Sherman turned to us. 'Young love, I don't know!' She laughed gaily.

I tried to my best to kill the conversation, suggesting we grab our seats, but there was no stopping Tyrone's mother now.

'Don't tell me you hadn't heard,' she said to my parents. 'Ty and Sam are an item.'

'An item of what?' This was my mother.

'An item as in together – a couple.' Mrs Sherman smiled proudly. 'Honestly, they're so secretive, these kids.'

'They are?' said Mr Burton.

'Tyrone is Sam's boyfriend. Aren't you, Ty?'

Mrs Sherman

I was slightly taken aback by how surprised the Burtons looked at the news I had just broken.

'It appears that my son has a reputation as something of a babe magnet,' I said, allowing a hint of motherly pride to enter my voice. 'The girls can't get enough of him. Especially darling little Sam.'

Tyrone groaned. 'Mum, please.'

'That's...interesting,' Mary Burton said in a slightly sniffy way.

'We'd better get to our seats,' added that little mouse of a husband of hers.

Smiling, I followed them. Did they really have to make it so obvious that they were jealous of me?

19

Matthew

We were in the final countdown before the gig started. The hall was filling up, but we found some places four rows from the front. We sat in line, three families, seven people and more secrets than you could count, as the audience settled down for the performance.

The evening had not started well. And it was just about to get a whole lot worse.

Ottoleen

We're late, can you believe it? All that waiting around and hanging out and we all but miss the danged thing.

It's what to wear that's the problem. Crash has this thing about blending in. He's been talking all week about us looking like real Brits and he's been so busy fussing in front of the mirror at the hotel that we only just make it to the show.

But we've done a good job. The way we look, no one can tell that we're anything but a nice young British couple checking out a school for their little kid.

All we have to do now is find out where Sam is.

Matthew

I felt my mother squeeze my arm. With wide-eyed, wordless panic, she nodded in the direction of the door.

There, framed in the doorway and looking about as out of place as anyone could be, were Mr and Mrs Lopez. Crash was in this blazer yachtsman-type thing, but spoiled the effect by wearing dark gangster shades. Mrs Lopez, in a flowery skirt and big hat, looked like she had walked straight out of an old movie.

'What are they doing here?' I whispered. 'They don't even know that Sam's at Bradbury Hill.'

More heads were turning as Crash and his wife made their way to a couple of spare seats in the third row.

'It's going to be all right.' Dad stared at the stage, his face pale. 'Sam's a girl.'

'Yeah, right,' I muttered. 'That's just fine then.'

The lights were dimmed. Mrs Cartwright left her seat in the VIP row at the front of the hall and climbed the steps on to the stage. Talent Night was about to begin.

Mrs Cartwright

It is an evening that is all about the kids, but I like to make what I call my mark on the evening by welcoming visitors, saying a few words about the school, noting some of our recent achievements, then leaving it to the young performers.

Matthew

Here's the way a Carthorse speech goes. First she tells you what she's going to say. Then she says it. Then she says it again, in slightly different words. Then, to finish off, she reminds you what she's been saying. Once she gets to her feet with that big queen-of-the-heap smile on her face, you just know that you're in for the long haul.

So I drifted off pretty quickly while she was giving us the usual message about how talented the kids were, how amazing and understanding the teachers were, how Bradbury Hill had just got better and better ever since she had arrived — prizes, grades, achievement, success — but I tuned back in when, glancing at a piece of paper in her hand, she said that there was a change to the programme.

'Zia Khan, one of Steve Forresters' stars of Year Eight — and I must say that Year Eight has been particularly impressive this term — will not now be singing solo but will be joined on stage by three other girls from her class in a band called...'

Elena

The *Pandas*?
We must have been in shock when, sitting in the

classroom a few minutes before the gig started, we agreed to that name.

'It's part of a whole concept.' Sam reached into the pocket of his jacket and took out a lighter, then an old cork. 'Everyone's going to notice my black eye, right?'

'It's kind of hard to miss,' said Charley.

Sam flicked the lighter and held it beneath the cork. 'So we turn it to our advantage,' he said. After a few seconds, he held up the blackened tip of the cork. 'We all have black eyes – like we've just come out of a fight.'

'Er, am I missing something here?' I said, trying to keep the sarcasm out of my voice. 'Why exactly would we want to do that?'

'It's funny. It's interesting. It solves the name problem. It's a statement.'

'A statement that we've totally lost it,' said Charley.

'Why not?' said Zia, who was tuning her guitar. 'I've seen pictures of models in Paris with fake black eyes. I've heard that it's really fashionable this year, the beaten-up look.'

'The beaten-up look. Yeah, I think I've read something about that in *Heat*.' I held out my hand. 'OK, gimme the cork,' I said.

Matthew

For some reason, can't think why, I remember very little of the first hour of the show. A couple of kids from Year Seven sawed away at violins. A four-piece band from the Lower Sixth stood on stage looking moody as they did a couple of cover versions of recent hits. A guy from the year above me went through a comic routine about parents, which seemed mostly to consist of him asking us, 'What's that all about, eh? Eh?' A few inhabitants of the Planet Nerd from my year did a couple of African choir songs. In between each turn, the Carthorse lumbered on stage to introduce the next act.

I was in a semi-snooze when I heard the head make the announcement our little part of the audience had been waiting for. 'And now, ladies and gentleman, it's time for a bit of wildlife – and I mean wild life! – with the Pandas!'

Elena, Charley, Zia and then Sam shambled on to the stage. There was soot stuff on their arms and faces and Sam had torn the sleeve of his shirt. They looked like survivors from a bomb blast.

For a moment or two, a shocked silence hung in the air. What was going on here? Was it some kind of satire thing? Then, good old Mrs Sherman started clapping and going 'Very good'. The audience laughed uneasily, and Zia struck the first chord of 'Private Cloud'.

Something happened when Sam began to sing that night. A sort of shudder ran through the audience as if suddenly they were all caught up in the moment, snatched out of their mood of polite boredom and pulled in by the sound of Sam's voice and Zia's guitar.

'They say – don't let your heart rule your head, But I say – you're gonna be a long time dead.' So relaxed that he seemed almost to be having a conversation with himself, Sam reached out a hand as the music built to the chorus. 'I feel my life slip like water through the fingers of my hand, And I'll be high in the sky—'

But at that moment, as Zia harmonised the chorus, a problem became apparent. There was nothing else for the other two Pandas to do during the song except jiggle around in the background. Charley swayed about, looking like she was drunk or something while Elena, perhaps because by now no one had paid any attention to her for several seconds, went into a look-at-me dance routine.

The mood was broken. There was barely suppressed laughter from the audience. I looked down the row and caught Jake's eye. He crossed his eyes and drew a finger across his throat.

Steve Forrester

I was impressed. I knew that Zia Khan had musical talent, but Sam Lopez was a revelation. That voice – angry yet strangely tender – had real quality. It was haunting, different.

I admit I was at something of a loss to understand the significance of why they were called the 'Pandas'. Only later did I begin to understand the subtle message that they were putting over. The black eyes, the bruises – it was nothing less than a savage, teenage perspective of the problem of domestic violence.

Brilliant. I was chuffed to bits. Dead proud of my girls, I was.

Matthew

The Pandas finished 'Private Cloud'. During the applause, led by Mrs Sherman, who seemed about to explode with pride at her son's girlfriend, I noticed that Sam was eyeing the audience.

He smiled at Jake and his father, at Tyrone and his mum, he winked at me. Then, I noticed something change and harden in his expression.

Sam gazed down at the third row. There, staring up at him, he saw the unmistakable, blazered figure of his dad, Mr Crash Lopez.

Crash

'It's the kid we saw round at the Burtons,' I said.

'She's way talented,' said Ottoleen.

'I guess,' I said. 'For a Canadian.'

We laughed at my joke and it was then that I noticed that the kid was still staring at us, kinda mean and hostile. For a nanosecond I wondered what her problem was. Then I thought nothing more of it.

Matthew

There was this weird silence that filled the hall and seemed to go on for minutes as Sam eyeballed his dad while the other Pandas stood around looking awkward.

Were they going to sing another number? Was someone meant to be giving it some verbals between numbers? Or were they just cranking up the tension? Either way, it worked. There were murmurings in the audience, a bit of nervous laughter.

Mrs Cartwright, maybe sensing that something was going wrong with her precious Talent Night, stood up as if she were about to step on to the stage and introduce the next act.

Sam slowly turned his eyes towards her. 'Hit it, Zed,' he said into the microphone, and Zia struck the face of her guitar like she was something out of a heavy-metal band. It was a hard, banging beat – angrier and faster than the last song.

It was also very, very loud.

Zia

We had worked on the songs, but none of us had thought about how we should get from 'Private Cloud' to 'Bad Girl'.

Looking back now, I can see that Sam's broody staring act was better than any lame intro, but at the time we were all sweating with embarrassment and nerves. What the hell was Sam doing?

During the awkward silence I must have fiddled with the volume knob on my guitar because, when I played the opening chords, the noise almost blew us off the stage.

I was aware of two things – that the audience was looking up at us, wide-eyed and scared, and that there was no way that I could stop and start again.

So 'Bad Girl' was coming at them like a runaway train – and that was before Sam started singing.

Matthew

A strange vibe had kicked in by now and everyone in the hall was aware of it.

Sam stepped forward a couple of paces, planted his feet a few inches apart as if he were squaring up for a fight, fixed his eyes a few feet over the audience's heads and began to sing.

No, come to think of it, sing is the wrong word. It wasn't a shout either. The sound that Sam made was something else, something beyond music and beyond the words that he sang, something that felt like pure, beautiful rage, something that had been gouged out of his soul with a rusty knife.

'My momma says be pretty, girl
My poppa's on my case.
Like, am I a doll or a member
Of the freakin' human race?
Everyday they come on like
I'm the family disgrace.
Hey, Mummy, Hey, Daddy
Just get out of my face.'

Mrs Cartwright

Frankly, it was not what Talent Night was meant to be about, this bloodcurdling noise coming from the stage. I'm almost sure I heard the Lopez child say 'freaking'. Was this a swear word? It sounded very much like one. I turned to Mr Brownlow, the town councillor who was on my right, and tried to apologise. Of course, he couldn't hear a word I was saying.

Elena

We knew what was happening was different from rehearsals. This was a new Sam, a Sam that was lifting us, pulling the music along. It was scary but amazing.

Matthew

Don't ask me how the audience reacted during the song. I couldn't take my eyes off Sam. I was mesmerised by him, and my guess is that everybody else was mesmerised too.

This was true rage, a musical version of what every kid in that place had felt at some time but most of us had never dared to say, let alone sing out loud, in public.

Fists clenched by his side, Sam hit the second verse.

> *'Me, I'm just me*
> *Not some crazy kind of creature*
> *But when I go to school*

I get hassle from the teacher
She says that when there's trouble
She just knows I'm gonna feature
She's, "Heaven knows, I try my best
But I just cannot what I call reach her"!'

Whoa, this was dangerous. Sam spat out the lines in a perfect, unmistakable imitation of Mrs Cartwright. A sort of unbelieving cheer came from the kids who knew just what was going on.

Mrs Cartwright

I was aware that at the end of the second verse a few heads turned in my direction. I smiled and kept tapping my hand on my leg in time with the beat. Clearly the girls were not referring to anyone in particular but to teachers utterly unlike those we have at Bradbury Hill – old-fashioned authority figures. I was not pleased by their general attitude, but decided to smile through it.

Matthew

The joke on Carthorse seemed to snap the audience out of its trance. Suddenly, we were no longer afraid or embarrassed by what was happening on stage. We could enjoy it – for the first time in history, an act on Talent Night was telling it like it really was, rather than like parents and teachers would like it to be.

When the three girls came in on the chorus, shouting it at us, we started clapping in time to the beat.

> *'Bad girl, bad girl.*
> *With a bad kind of fame.*
> *For being the baddest of the bad*
> *Bad girl is my name.'*

Charley

We had a choice to make. Either to sing the chorus in the tight, neat way that Zia had written it and we had practised it, or to follow Sam into whatever place he had gone.

We followed. The result may have sounded more like a football chant than a song, but it worked. By the end of the first chorus, the audience was going wild.

Matthew

The Pandas were well into it now. Charley and Elena were doing their dance, Zia was going at her guitar like a mad axe-man. But the greater the mayhem all round him, the stiller Sam stood. It was funny but frightening, because no one – maybe not even Sam himself – knew how seriously he was taking it all.

> *'The boys all try to hit on me*
> *"Let's go clubbin out tonight"*
> *They tell me I'm a babe*

I'm such a pretty sight.
But when we hit the High Street
They find out too right
This baby ain't for dancin'
This baby wants to fight!'

Mrs Cartwright

Enough. Enough. I stood up, looking for the caretaker to switch off the sound, but then to my horror I realised that the audience had stood up too. They actually thought I was giving the girls a standing ovation.

I had no alternative but to go along with it, sway and clap with the rest of them, but I swore to myself that this would never ever be permitted to happen at a Bradbury Hill Talent Night again.

Ottoleen

Hey, rock and roll, baby! I'm screaming at Crash that suddenly this is like the best gig since I caught the New York Dolls at CBGBs, but he's still sitting down like Mr Straight from Straightville, Arizona, while all around him these kids are going totally wild.

So eventually Crash slowly gets to his feet, raises his big, muscular arms above his head and screams, 'Yay, Bad Girls, go for it!' and I'm laughing like I'm fit to bust.

I tell you, those kids are really good.

Zia

I was kind of chuffed by the way it was going. 'Bad Girl' was my song and, on its first performance, it was lifting the roof off. There was one more verse – the one about us all being bad girls coming good. Then there would be a chorus, replayed once; a shock staccato ending and we were out of there.

I hadn't reckoned on any surprises from our lead singer. When we reached the last verse, Sam did something weird with the vocals – he went up a third as if harmonising with himself so that his voice was now high and strained and angry.

There was something else. He replaced my words with his.

Matthew

I noticed a change in Sam. He seemed to relax as the song progressed. As they were singing one of the choruses he looked down at me squarely, then at Mum and Dad, and gave the merest hint of a smile. Then his eyes moved down the line and fixed on Crash Lopez. There they stayed until the song came to its spectacular end.

> *'I'm a dawg, all you people*
> *I'm danger on the prowl*
> *On the street, in the heat*
> *In the gutters mean and foul*
> *Hear my bark, feel my bite*

Hear my wolverine growl.
Smell my dawg-breath,
Daddy, And listen to me—'

Crash

And as the kid said 'dog-breath, Daddy', she pointed her finger straight at me. I was like, hey, what *is* this?

Matthew

'Hooooooooo—'

As Zia, Charley and Elena and some of the audience hit the 'Bad girl, bad girl' chorus, Sam's voice soared up and up.

'Ooooooooooooo—'

It was unlike anything I've heard – wilder than Scooby-Doo, spookier than the Hound of the Baskervilles, beyond the scariest wolf noise you ever heard. Now and then he took a quick breath, then carried on howling.

There was laughter at first. But when the Pandas reached the end of the chorus, they looked at one another and their uncertainty reached the audience. Now there was tension in the air. The clapping and chanting died down, Zia's rhythm guitar faltered, then stopped.

Sam kept going. He took one more deep breath and hit an even higher note as if he were trying to push his voice to breaking point.

And suddenly I knew what was going to happen.

Tyrone

There was a sort of catch in Sam's voice, a violent croaking in the throat. He hesitated, coughed, took a deep breath and—

Jake

Uh-oh.

Elena

Oh...my...God.

Crash

What the—?

Matthew

It wasn't a howl that came from Sam now but a roar – deep, throaty and unmistakably male.

There were mutterings, the sound of nervous laughter in the hall.

But Sam wasn't finished. He walked to the front of the stage. Staring deep into the eyes of his father, he raised the microphone to his mouth and growled, slowly and deliberately in his brand-new, masculine voice, the words, 'Bad guy is my name.'

'It's a boy.' The word spread like a bush fire through the audience – 'a boy…a guy…she's a he…a boy.'

I glanced over at the head teacher, but, for the first time in living memory, she was completely lost for words, as stunned as the rest of us.

Elena

Somebody had to take control of the situation and at that moment I decided it had to be Elena Griffiths. We needed to get off stage somehow, so I stepped forward, took the microphone from Sam and said, 'Thank you, everyone. We were the Pandas. Let's hear it for guitarist Zia Khan and our lead singer—'

Jake

No.

Tyrone

No!

Matthew

No, Elena!

Elena

'—Sam Lopez!'

Jake

The audience was about to start applauding when there was this mighty roar from the third row.

Crash

'THAT'S MY SON!'

Matthew

A few yards away from me, Crash Lopez was blundering towards the stage, pushing past other members of the audience, pointing at Sam, bellowing out the truth.

Sam looked down at him and, for a moment, I saw an expression on his face that I had never ever seen before. It was one of fear.

He turned and made for the exit at the back of the stage.

As pandemonium broke out in the hall, I turned to my parents, who were staring, spooked and ashen, at the door through which Sam had just disappeared.

'I think it's time we did some explaining,' I said.

Mrs Cartwright

It was what I call a crisis situation. After a hurried discussion with Mrs Sparks, the teacher coordinating Talent Night, I announced that the rest of the event was abandoned and that the remaining two acts would perform at our Christmas play.

The audience was dispersing, but I still had an irate American to deal with. My first reaction was that the man was delusional, but, when he produced a wallet with a number of brightly coloured credit cards, each bearing the name 'Lopez', I had to accept that there was the possibility of a family connection with the girl – who now turned out to be a boy – Sam Lopez.

I took the American couple and Mr and Mrs Burton to my study, leaving Matthew to sit outside.

There I told them in no uncertain terms that this was a family matter and that it was not for Bradbury Hill School to become involved in what was thoroughly what I call inappropriate.

Ottoleen

'In a what?' goes Crash, standing in the middle of the principal's study. She's behind her desk looking like someone made a smell under her nose. The Burtons are sitting nearby, all nervous and pale and English.

'Inappropriate,' goes the starchy old bird, who's looking kind of freaked now on account of Crash leaning on her desk, fists down, giving her the eyeball. 'I do not wish the school to become involved in this issue.'

'Oh, the school is involved, believe me, lady,' says Crash, more quietly now. 'When you have my son at your school, on stage, dressed up as a girl, you are most certainly involved.' He points a finger. 'You fetch my son right now, we take him back where he belongs and maybe, just maybe, I won't tell the cops about this.'

Mrs Cartwright

Frankly, it seemed a sensible suggestion, even if the threatening tone was not something I welcomed. The last thing I needed, just when my career was going so well, was a scandal involving an American child who had been taken from his home and didn't know whether he was a boy or a girl.

'I'll ask my secretary to fetch him,' I said quietly, picking up the phone.

Mrs Burton

Suddenly David did something which I never would have expected. He stood up, placed a finger on the telephone's receiver and said in a voice that was really quite manly, 'No.'

Sam's hooligan father continued staring at Mrs Cartwright, 'Make the call, lady,' he said.

'No.' My husband stood his ground. 'We have been given responsibility over Sam and, if this is his father, he should take his claim to a court of law.'

Mr Lopez turned his head slowly so that his nose was almost touching David's. 'Maybe the kid should decide about that.'

'Maybe he should,' said David.

Mrs Cartwright looked at the two men, then down at her telephone, on which David was still holding his finger. Sighing, she stood up and went to the door. She opened it and said, 'Matthew, would you be so kind as to fetch Sam Lopez?'

I heard Matthew saying, 'Yes, Mrs Cartwright.'

The head teacher returned to her desk and sat down.

'This is all very unfortunate,' she said.

Matthew

There was quite a crowd when I walked into the classroom. Jake and Tyrone, with Mr Smiley and Mrs Sherman, were there, so were Mr and Mrs Khan and a couple of the younger Khan children. Elena was with her mum, who was standing near to Mr and Mrs Johnson, Charley's parents.

For the briefest second, I forgot about the whole Sam drama. Here they all were, mixing and chatting, not like parents on the one side, kids on the other, boys against girls, Sheds v Bitches, but just...families. Weird.

Then I saw Sam.

He was still in a skirt, but someone had lent him a white school shirt to put over his bare shoulders and his hair was hanging over his face in true hippy fashion. At that moment, he looked neither entirely boy nor girl – just sad, confused and lost.

'They're in Carthorse's, office,' I said to him. 'They want to see you.'

Sam stood up. Zia muttered, 'Good luck,' as he made his way to the door, walking like a man going to his execution. He raised a weary hand in acknowledgement.

'So much for Operation Samantha,' he said, his voice hoarse, as we reached the corridor.

'Yup,' I said. 'It looks like your girly days are over.'

'I couldn't help it,' said Sam. 'I saw him, sitting there, the big smile on his face, just like it used to be when we were all together. And I knew, in my gut and in my heart, that I had to stop running away. The moment had arrived. It was time to be me.'

'You want to go back to your father?'

Sam shrugged. It seemed that he wasn't in the mood for conversation. We had reached the door to the head's study and, without knocking, he pushed his way in.

I hesitated for a moment, then followed.

Ottoleen

Crash checks out who's walked into the office and sees that the English boy Matthew is standing behind Sam. 'Lose the kid,' he says.

'This involves Matthew as well,' says Mrs Burton. 'Sam?' says the principal. 'Do you want Matthew here or not?'

Sam has been staring at the ground like he's looking for the answer to his problems in the pattern of the carpet. Now he looks up. 'Sure I do,' he says.

Elena

We tried to behave normally, chatting about this and that in the classroom. One of the parents – Tyrone's mum – suggested that we might all go out for a pizza together, but there was no way that we could leave Sam and Matthew battling it out with Psycho Dad and his girlfriend in Carthorse's study.

So, after a while, we drifted out to the school lobby and waited for them outside the head's study.

Mrs Cartwright

I addressed the rather peculiar gathering that was now in my study. I explained that in no way was Bradbury Hill responsible for any family misunderstandings or conflicts that occurred outside school premises, but that I had agreed that it would be sensible if some kind of resolution was found so that, at the very least, the child Lopez knew who she (he) was going home with tonight.

In my coolest tone, I asked, 'Would someone care to explain how I came to have an American child in my school who has no contact with his father and who has been disguised as a girl since the beginning of term?'

Matthew

There was a beat of silence. Then Mum started talking. She told the whole story. The way she explained it, there was no great deal in what had happened. It was just one of those crazy family situations.

Crash

I've knocked around a bit in my time, but I swear to you I have never heard such a load of baloney in all my days.

'Lemme get this straight, I spoke in my quiet, snake-about-to-strike tone. 'You come over to my ex-wife's funeral and, just because I happened not to be around at the time, you take away my son. Right? Out of his country. Away from his family. Am I missing something so far?'

Mrs Burton gave me the cold English look that I now knew so well. 'It was my sister's wish. She thought you were still in jail. She believed that we could give her son a sound and stable family background.'

'Let me just remind you of one small detail.' I spoke casually, then exploded. *'He's been dressed up in a goddam skirt for the last three weeks!* Is that your idea of a sound and stable family background?'

'It's plain dysfunctional is what it is,' said Ottoleen. 'You've probably messed that poor kid up for life. He won't know if he's Sam or' – she hesitated for a moment – 'Samette…Samine…Samma?'

The cream-puff-fink Burton looks at Ottoleen like she's some kind of basket case. Then he turns to me. 'Is Sam really more messed up than when he was living with Mr Lopez? Somehow I doubt it. And I have to ask whether Sam's inheritance has anything to do with—'

I had heard enough. 'He's my kid,' I hollered. 'I'm taking him home.'

I thumped the desk. Hard.

Matthew

The sound of Crash's fist on the desk seemed to bring Sam out of his trance. For the first time since we walked into the office, he looked, direct and unblinking, at his father.

'Do you remember the wall?' he asked quietly.

'Wall?' Crash narrowed his eyes threateningly. 'What are you talkin' about?'

'The wall where I saw you for the last time. The wall that changed my life.'

Crash glanced over at Mrs Cartwright. 'I told you that putting the kid in drag would mess up his mind.' He turned back to Sam. 'We'll talk about the old times later, son,' he said, a hint of threat in his voice.

'Tell us about the wall, Sam,' said my father.

'I had just turned five,' said Sam, his eyes still fixed on Crash. 'You had been taking me out on jobs for a few months already. You called me "Crash Junior". You said I was one of the gang.'

'Happy days,' said Crash nervously.

'Dare one ask what kind of job this was?' asked Mrs Cartwright.

As if no one else was in the room except him and his father, Sam continued. 'This job was special, you said. It was a chance to prove that I was a real tough guy, just like my daddy. All I had to do was to stand on a ledge outside a second-floor window where you put me. Then, after I had counted to a hundred, you wanted me to step out on to a wall that was overlooking the main drag, walk out a few steps and start screaming, just as loud as I could. All the folks down there would panic, right? No one would notice that, on the corner of the street, three guys were walking in to help themselves to a payroll bag as it was delivered to a shop.'

'Help themselves?' It seemed that Mrs Cartwright was beginning to understand what this was all about.

'It was a good plan,' said Sam. 'After all, the wall was thirty feet above the concrete sidewalk. Seeing a small kid up there alone would be a pretty good diversion, right?'

'Twenty-five feet, they said in court,' Crash muttered.

'But I blew it,' said Sam. 'I looked down and suddenly I felt dizzy. I really did panic. I screamed and screamed and then I pointed to you and called out to you again and again when I saw you pull in to the side of the street in the getaway car. Except you didn't get away.'

There was silence in the office as we waited for Sam's father to speak.

'Poor Sam,' my mother murmured.

We looked at Crash Lopez. Suddenly he was no longer this hard billiard ball of a guy. He rolled his shoulders uneasily. 'It wasn't your fault, kid,' he said. 'It was mine. I was young. You were scared of the wall, but I was scared too – scared of drowning in family life, losing my freedom, losing everything that mattered to me. Go and grab the world by the throat – that's the Crash Lopez way.'

'And that's what you're doing now,' said Sam.

'It's not the money, I swear,' said Crash. 'I thought the million bucks was what mattered to me when I flew over here, but now I've seen you, I feel differently.'

'What money?' asked Mrs Cartwright. 'Would someone kindly tell me what is going on here?

'You never came back to see us,' said Sam. 'All my life, I've believed that I was the reason you ended up in jail.'

'Listen, kid. Things were kinda complicated. There were people who wanted to see me real bad – people who did not have my best interests at heart, if you know what I mean. I didn't want to get you and Galaxy involved.'

'Bull,' said Sam. 'You were living your life'. A flicker of a glance took in Ottoleen: 'Having fun. And you know what? I don't blame you. Maybe I'll do the same thing one day.'

Crash chuckled uneasily. 'Chip off the old—'

'You didn't want me around. You only wanted me when I was useful. Recently I've discovered that not everyone's like that.'

Crash shrugged uneasily. 'Hey, I was young. I was out of my depth. I've changed, kid. I've got feelings deep down where it matters.'

'Yeah?' Sam smiled sadly. 'I doubt if Crash Lopez will have real, true family feelings for as long as he lives.'

There was silence for a moment. Then, something very strange – even stranger than what was already happening – took place. A sort of weird police-siren-like wail came from Ottoleen.

'He has got family feelings,' she managed to say eventually. 'He's like this totally big-time father kind of guy.'

'You weren't there,' said Sam.

Ottoleen glanced down at him. 'I'm not talking about you, you little jerk,' she snapped. 'You've been nothing but trouble. We only wanted you back because of the cash. I'm talking about his real family.'

Everyone stared at her. 'What exactly are you saying, Ottoleen?' Crash asked.

'Our baby.' Ottoleen put a hand on her stomach. 'Just promise me you'll have family feelings towards our baby, Crash.'

'Are you saying you're pregnant?'

Ottoleen nodded and smiled gloopily through her tears. 'I took the test yesterday. I didn't know when to break it to you,' she whispered. 'All you could think about was this brat of yours.'

And Crash opened his arms and let his sobbing wife

walk into a big, gentle bear hug.

'Baby, baby, baby,' he said. 'I'm so proud of my little kitten.'

Ottoleen, face against Crash's chest, was making a strange new noise.

'Miew,' she went. 'Miew, mieeeeew.'

I looked across at Sam. He shook his head. In spite of the craziness and the stress, in spite of everything, we started laughing.

Charley

The noises that were coming from that office! Murmured conversation, then a bit of bawling and shouting, then quiet again, then a sort of high-pitched whine. I was agog to know what the hell was going on.

Then, just as we thought that this mad soap opera was going to last all night, the door to the head teacher's study opened.

Matthew

Sam and I stepped out first. There, to our amazement, was a small crowd, waiting for us in the school lobby.

For a second or two, there was silence as the two of us stood, framed by the doorway. Then I put an arm around Sam's shoulder and we both smiled.

I guess that must have said it all, because suddenly they were all applauding like we were back in Talent

Night and we had just completed some kind of brilliant performance.

Then, out of the crowd, this small figure rushed forward and threw her arms around Sam's neck.

Zia

Yes! Oh yes!

Matthew

All hell broke loose. The Lopezes came out of the study crying, the head was shouting to restore order, Mrs Khan was trying to pull Zia away from Sam, Mrs Sherman seemed to be having some kind of row with Tyrone, perhaps on account of his famous girlfriend having turned out to be a boy, Charley and Elena were standing with Jake and his dad, who was looking confused as they tried to talk him through precisely how all this had happened. It was going to take some explaining.

I stepped back and watched them for while. Across the lobby, my parents smiled. Mum gave me a double thumbs-up sign.

And, just for a couple of seconds, I almost lost it there and then. The whole scene became blurred, I felt this whole lump thing happening in my throat and a pricking around my eyes.

I cleared my throat, sniffed, squared my shoulders and walked towards them.

If this story was a Doors song, which would it be?

'Strange Days'?

'Ship of Fools'?

'Take It As It Comes'?

'Wild Child'?

You want my opinion, it would be a little number called 'Break on Through to the Other Side'.

Mr and Mrs Lopez broke on through by becoming Mom and Pop to a little girl called Elizabeth, named after the queen of the country where she started her journey into the world. Crash is Tony these days. He's the proprietor of My Private Cloud, a restaurant in downtown Santa Barbara.

Matthew, Elena, Tyrone, Charley and Jake broke on through to something which looks suspiciously like friendship. They discovered what some folks take a lifetime to learn – that there's no point in fighting the difference between guys and girls. In fact, maybe it's the difference that makes life kind of weird and interesting.

At least, sometimes. When it comes to Sam Lopez, he's broken on through to the other side in his own way. Sometimes, just to mix things up a bit, he likes to go out as Samantha. Folks can be different even in one body, he had discovered. Summers he flies over to the States to see his dad and his stepfamily out on the coast. The rest of the year he's living in London with his new gang, with the Burtons, with Zia, singing songs, living life out loud.

It may sound like a mess, but sometimes mess can be OK, mess can be fine. Sometimes mess is just another word for living your life as the real you, not someone else's version of what they think you should be.

And, take it from me, that feels good.

WE ARE ALL MADE OF MOLECULES

A NOVEL BY SUSIN NIELSEN

Longlisted for the Carnegie Medal

Stewart is geeky, gifted but socially clueless. His mom has died and he misses her every day. Ashley is popular, cool but her grades stink. Her dad has come out and moved out – but not far enough.

Their worlds are about to collide: Stewart and his dad are moving in with Ashley and her mom. Stewart is 89.9% happy about it even as he struggles to fit in at his new school. But Ashley is 110% horrified and can't get used to her totally awkward home. And things are about to get a whole lot more mixed up when they attract the wrong kind of attention. . .

'Snappy and witty. A really fine YA novel' *Telegraph*

'I defy you not to fall in love with this book' *Phil Earle*

9781783443765   £7.99

The Absolutely True Diary of a Part-Time INDIAN

SHERMAN ALEXIE

A NEW YORK TIMES BESTSELLER

WINNER OF THE NATIONAL BOOK AWARD

'Son, you're going to find more and more hope the farther and farther you walk away from this sad, sad reservation.'

So Junior, a budding cartoonist, who is already beaten up regularly for being a skinny kid with glasses, decides to go to the rich all-white high school miles away. He'll be a target there as well, but he hopes he'll also get a chance to prove everyone wrong. This is the incredible story of one Native American boy as he attempts to break away from the life he thought he was destined to live.

'Excellent in every way'
Neil Gaiman

'Overflows with truth, pain and black comedy'
New York Times

9781783442010

EVERYBODY JAM

ALI LEWIS

Shortlisted for the Carnegie Medal

Danny Dawson lives in the middle of the Australian outback. His older brother Jonny was killed in an accident last year but no one ever talks about it.

And now it's time for the annual muster. The biggest event of the year on the cattle station, and a time to sort the men from the boys. But this year things will be different: because Jonny's gone and Danny's determined to prove he can fill his brother's shoes; because their fourteen-year-old sister is pregnant; because it's getting hotter and hotter and the rains won't come; because cracks are beginning to show . . .

'What an incredible debut. Lewis brings rough poetry and raw poignancy to this coming-of-age tale. I loved it.' Keith Gray, author of *Ostrich Boys*

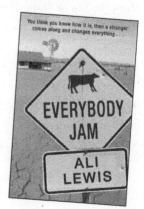

9781849392488 £7.99